No More Reunions

No More Reunions

JOHN BOWERS

E. P. DUTTON & CO., INC. | NEW YORK | 1973

Published simultaneously in Canada by
Clarke, Irwin & Company Limited, Toronto and Vancouver
SBN: 168052
Library of Congress Catalog Card Number: 72-94688

For T.R.B., Howard, Mochy,
and C.M.

One

What continued to throw me was, I could see no justice in his beating me. He was a newcomer to the poolroom while I was a veteran of a good year's standing. I could hold the cue stick in the crook of my forefinger with my thumb gently supporting it, my three fingers splayed out the way the big boys did it. He still shot with his hand cupped down, using the small crevice between thumb and first knuckle as the bridge for the cue. Strictly for beginners. And he flew around the table, eager and quick, just giving his cue tip a flick of blue chalk. Goddamnit, you were supposed to ponder your shots, stand back and keep throwing your eye between the cue ball and numbered balls, screeching your cue tip all the while with chalk. His way was like running out on a basketball court and beginning the game furiously, with no warm-up, no "Star-Spangled Banner," in your street clothes. You weren't supposed to be that hungry.

This was Pancho MacAfee, and he lived down the block from me. We called him "Pancho" (his real name was Clarence) because the first thing you noticed about him was that he was darker than most—with eyes like pieces of coal and hair that turned bluish-black in the light. There was hardly a time when I couldn't remember him. Before we were six we had both learned how to swim at the Maple Street Pool. Even now I can still see, as if yesterday, his frowning face as he hovered on the wet plank walk, at the edge of the mysterious green water, his arms outstretched stiffly, hands together, his baggy bathing trunks nearly falling, looking as if he might be strangled by plunging in. I enjoyed his look of fear for I was diving in then from a full trot with an accompanying series of whoops. I was hoping that his girl cousin, Mary Sue, who had his same dark hair and eyes, might notice—or that blonde girl who kept her hair under a rubber bathing cap. Even then I gloried in the frills, the preliminaries, the *warm-up* instead of the real basic thing. Later I was to be called a romantic for it.

And so as the years progressed I still dived from the same short run, the same quick splash. But Pancho. Suddenly, inexplicably one summer he began doing flips from the board and then one of those impossible gainers. He still held that same determined frown as he waited his turn, but then he raced out, flipped backward and disappeared in the deep. He could even do a *one-and-a-half*. And where he learned that I'll never know. It was as if it had just been waiting to come out —like all those other strange things that began happening. You would know some boy with alabaster complexion for years and the next moment his face would be aflame with pimples. And in the shower you could see someone you'd always thought of as a friend, someone who'd never tried any tricks on you, who had always been more or less like you, who'd suddenly come up with a wang on him that went down to his knees. That really killed you. Particularly when all you had were a few sprouts of hair that only seemed destined to cover the works. We called the moment in life "getting the hairs." It was a big moment in Tennessee.

The bathroom at home was our one spot of privacy, where we could examine ourselves morning, noon, and night in the hopes of additional hairs and just a little lengthening of the tool. I stood and caught the picture from the old mirror over the basin. There was the shot from the side, where, when you pressed in on your stomach, the thing didn't seem too much a dwarf. Nineteenth or twentieth examination of the day completed, it was into still another ice-cold bath, which brought on tonsillitis but kept the tool from rising. For my father had taken me into the unused barn out back one day— scary just by itself—and said, "Don't ever play with yourself, son. Ninety-five percent of the people in insane asylums are there because of that. It's a fact." And on page 448 of the *Boy Scout Manual,* under Conservation, it said,

. . . no steps should be taken to excite seminal emissions. That is masturbation. It is a bad habit. It should be fought against. It's something to keep away from. Keep control in sex matters. It's manly to do so. It's important for one's life, happiness, efficiency, and the whole human race as well. [*On and on, God!*] Keep in training. A cold hip bath will help, water temperature 56° to 60° F., sitting in a tub, feet out, fifteen minutes at night before going to bed.

Every time a warmness threatened to spread down there, I would say, Get away from me, devil. I'm going to become a man! But disaster waited nearly everywhere at anytime. When I

11

caught a glimpse of a woman teacher's rolled garter, I almost lost consciousness. Even a cowboy movie was fraught with danger after awhile, for somewhere among the shooting and fistfights and herds of cattle would come a pretty and intense woman. What did it matter if she wore a bonnet and had a gingham dress that went down to her ankles? There was the *outline* of tits and a great big butt. Oh God, help me to be normal! Sometimes I wasn't able to get out of my seat fast enough, the girl's smile would blossom too quickly, a flash of cleavage would pop out of the blue, and the damn thing I was stuck with wouldn't listen to a word I said. Oh Lord, look out, I'm insane asylum bound! But out on the street, groggy but revived in the fierce sunlight, balls aching as if they had been wrung, I promised the Almighty that I wouldn't go against the Scriptures. And it looked to me that if I kept myself pure against so much temptation, the Lord might be inclined to do something for me, too. Like give me just one more inch.

Sleep didn't count. One wasn't responsible. And that was when the fireworks really began. The first explosion came usually a second or two after the head touched the pillow, following a perfunctory dream that gave it an excuse. Half-awakened, you would feel warm fluid run down your leg and wet whatever garment covered you at the moment—shorts, pajamas, long handles in freezing weather. In the middle of the night came the second firing, and sometime around reveille—often just as my mother called for breakfast—would go the final squirt. How unfair that I seldom got to dream of putting myself in a woman. There'd go my bare foot in warm mud or something and I'd lose another one. Nothing was safe or sacred in my diseased mind. Once the scenario had a lovely girl raise her skirt, and—lo and behold—she presented something that looked like male genitals. Good heavens, a mistake,

12

a mistake! So much gissum was flying—once I unloaded during an afternoon nap—that its aroma of chewed grass stayed with me through the day like a smoker's scent of tobacco. It shamed me terribly to have friends move away from me to far desks in class, but what could I do? You couldn't beat back all the assaults of come.

Night became such a juice-producing operation that finally I couldn't sleep. In bed I told myself, for hour after hour, Here I am dropping off. But nothing happened. Every time I neared the unconscious I awoke myself by thinking, This is it. And so through the day I moved, exhausted and bewildered. Had anyone else ever had such a problem? When I tried to explain to someone that I couldn't sleep anymore because I awoke each time at the crucial moment, reminding myself that it was about to happen, I was met with blank looks. My mother said I had a "tic." I tried warm milk, hot Ovaltine, warm baths, cold baths, going to bed at eight in the evening and staying up to midnight. Nothing worked. Until a sun-kissed afternoon in spring when I ran across a psychology book in the high school library. It must have got there by mistake. It said, way in the back, as if in afterthought,

Let us now have a word about masturbation. No one has determined how much harm the myths surrounding masturbation have caused. It does not bring on insanity, paralysis of the spine, or any of the other countless disabilities that have been attributed to it by misguided folkways. Masturbation is a phase that most boys and some girls go through to relieve the tensions of adolescence. If continued into adulthood—

But who cared about adulthood? We'd cross that bridge when we came to it.

And then, as if my good luck that afternoon knew no bounds, I ran across *My Son, My Son* in the fiction shelves.

Surely *it* had got there by mistake or else the librarian, Miss Georgia Ann Kyker, was holding a secret intelligence. She seemed only maniacally concerned that people not chew gum. On page 422, miracle of miracles, it read,

> She remained for a time rigid, almost resistant. Then my heat melted her. Her body relaxed and she gave me kiss for kiss. She herself threw off the overall she was wearing and thrust my hand up under the loose jumper to the warm flesh of her straining breast. She pressed herself against me, limb to limb, each limb alive and passionate. So this is Livia! She said huskily: "Lock the door." When I turned from doing so she was already pulling the jumper over her head.

Good God Almighty, women *do* it, they really do!

There was no way to miss the passage. The book fell open naturally there although it was two-thirds toward the end, the section much darker than pages around it, some words almost smudged out of existence. In case all other indications failed, it was dog-eared. Comments were scrawled in the margin: "Oh, wow!!!" and, "Boy, a good ole hore!" On the inside cover was the penciled message: "Check page 422. Man oh man!" Later, in any number of unrelated books, I found other messages about the delights of *My Son, My Son,* citing chapter and verse. There was even a note about it I discovered in the lavatory. Such brotherhood and thoughtfulness! We were like prisoners passing along vital and secret intelligence, all pointing toward escape.

I walked from school that day, taking the shortcut past a colored folks' shanty, up the hill, across the vacant lot, inside, and like a shot into the bathroom. From a side view in the old mirror, standing, I saw the cargo fly out and sail across the bathtub. Relief at last from blondes and big tits and the locomotives of cheerleaders. That night I slept like a baby. And from then on I had it on learned authority, down in black and white: It was just a way to relieve tension. So it had its "reason" and therefore its place and protocol and manners. Like the poolroom.

Now Pancho lined up his shot seriously in our nine-ball game. A blanket of light from twin dangling lamps lay over the worn, fading green table, and Pancho frowned from the shadows. It was around high noon, but could have been midnight that Saturday for all the sunlight that reached our back table. The real studs took the front tables, drawing crowds and playing for big money and being near the beer cooler. Pancho and I had fifteen cents down each, loser pays for the game. He kissed the three ball into the side, miscuing in the process. Then he chalked and pushed past me to line up on the four. I didn't like the way he brushed against me, too eager, no manners. He'd better watch himself there. And then he missed. I jiggled some talcum on my left hand from the creaky machine, shot my fist up and down the cue, and then chalked and chalked some more. Thinking of that fifteen cents caused my stomach to quiver. I brushed off the path between the cue ball and the four. Pancho kept frowning, not speaking. We usually had a steady chatter going, and his silence was a little unnerving. Lined up, aiming, I drew back, liking the feel of the smooth talcumed wood. "Don't miss," Pancho said.

"Piss."

I had to take aim all over again. And then I sank the four with a crisp, soul-satisfying snap into the leather of a corner pocket, working into excellent position on the five. That fell, too, with a soft nudge, the cue ball running to the center of the table. A hard session at chalking, in which I pretended to think. A bridge was called for here—that utensil kept ready at each table, like an extension for your pecker—to allow you to reach a far-off shot. But somehow it was sissy to use the bridge, as if you admitted to personal inadequacy. I chalked some more, already knowing what I was going to do.

"Shoot, Bones. Or have you gone into a trance?"

"O.K., O.K.!"

I hoisted myself up on the table, sitting, and positioned the cue for a shot behind my back. It was like throwing the ball from behind your back in basketball. Tricky and showing some daring. Yet we both knew that this shot was not all that important, that who ultimately sank the yellow-and-white nine ball—colored like a yellow jacket—won. That was nine ball, which had nine balls racked up at the start in a diamond figure. One player could make all eight balls, and then the other sink the nine and win. Nine ball was a big gambling game in the Buffalo Palace. It was what the big boys played.

From behind my back I made the green six, even throwing a little bottom English in to make the cue ball dance back. Then I banked in the red seven with a firm pop—after the chalking, the glancing, the couple of turns around the table. But now the preliminaries, the jockeying, the *warm-up* was over. I missed that goddamn son of a bitching eight ball straight in. "Shit tall mighty!"

Pancho just hunched over the table, feet turned in pigeon-toed, frowning, serious, and bounced the eight in; however, rolling to an impossible angle on the nine. What lousy form he showed, what an amateurish stance he took. Me, somebody who could whack them in from behind the back, I should win easily if there were any fairness. With no talking, a minimum of chalking, he tried a bank shot on the nine and missed by a hair. And there it was, that nine ball standing right before the gaping hole of a corner pocket. A perfect straight-in. The game, the fifteen cents, was just waiting for me to take. Pancho made as if to give up, to swipe the ball in with his hand, but didn't. "Want me to go through with it?" I said.

"Sure. You ain't quite won yet."

He stood behind the pocket, holding his cue stick with both hands. In a way I was shooting right into him. I tried to keep my eye on the cue ball, the nine, to stay away from any picture of him. I didn't want to think. I drew back, heard him clear his throat, and fired. The nine sank, followed crazily by the cue ball. *Scratched!* Son of a dirty bitch. A laugh erupted from Pancho, not a full-throated blast, but more a rough, ridiculing chuckle. I don't think I'd ever heard him laugh joyfully, letting himself really go. As he lined up on the nine, which now lay in the difficult position on the spot, I walked back and forth near him, whistling, singing, bopping my cue stick on the floor. He stopped, brushed off an imagined speck on the table, and then returned to teasing his cue tip near the ivory cue ball. His eye suddenly leveling in on the nine, my own cue banging harder on the floor now, he drew back and sent his stick home. In a blur the cue ball shot forward and struck the nine, making the yellow-and-white ball fly into the corner pocket in a loud, sickening snap. The cue ball ran up and down the table, happy not to have scratched. I had to hand over fifteen cents.

Then he wanted to double up, play for thirty cents. The loser was supposed to want to double up to get his money back. Didn't he know that? I settled on shooting for a quarter. He won. And after a few more games, I fell back all the way into permanent loser territory. I figured out how I would get an advance on my seventy-five-cent weekly allowance by telling my mother that someone had picked my pocket downtown. Then next week I would save twenty cents each day on my lunch money. That would shore my funds back up for more pool shooting, a movie, and a pack of sweet-tasting Hav-A-Tampas with the wooden tips. Losing made you a little sick as if somehow you'd been caught at something dirty —like found carrying fuck books in your pocket. You were unworthy and a show-off for thinking and acting in the beginning as if you had expected to win. I wanted to go off and be by myself, but Pancho wouldn't let me. He came up while I was sitting on the top of a bench at the front, my Thom McAn's on the seat. (That's how you sat at the poolroom, so you could watch the action; it made it a little rough on those who sat on the bench in the regular way.) "Boney, you choked. I knew you were going to. *Choked!*"

"Awwwww."

"Listen, Boney, seriously. You got to help me on my geometry lesson for Monday. I'm counting on you. I might fail otherwise."

"All right. O.K."

Be damned if I would, though. And, anyhow, we both knew this was just his way of making up to me. When had he ever cared about geometry lessons or grades? Those were lodestones of mine, having a mother and father who went over report cards with a magnifying glass. But this phase of losing was not unpleasant. He had to be cheerful around me, kid me, throw out a few lines to build my ego back up. When you won, you learned to do this. Besides, we were buddies.

Buddies. Being buddies meant you walked home together after school a lot, checked in every evening by phone, and found others always asking about the other one. "How's old Pancho doing?" It was pleasant—and somehow necessary— to always have a main buddy. He was someone to fill in those long, boring times when you had nothing to do, someone to test out jokes and routines on, and finally someone who offered a place as an escape hatch from home. Buddies could

18

visit each other's homes at any time. In fact, that was the real test for buddies. If somebody was your real buddy, you could drop by his home at any hour—with no invitation.

And Pancho's home was a marvelous relief from my own. He lived with his aunt and uncle, not his real folks, and somehow this made his living arrangement more like camping out than that of a regular home. In mine everything had a time and a place. Dinner of corn bread or biscuits, fat-backed beans, and some kind of meat was steaming on the round kitchen table every evening at six. *"Dinner!* Tell your father. Your aunt. Wash your hands." A parade through the bathroom, a meal taken mostly in silence except for my mother hopping to refill milk glasses or to bring on more biscuits, and then back glutted in a daze to the coziness of the living room. The house kept at a boiler-room ninety degrees in respect to my aunt's thin blood. My aunt Milly, my mother's sister, had lived with us—or us with her—since time immemorial in one of many such arrangements in town. In permanent residence there was nearly always somebody like a grandfather, a great grandfather, a loony brother or uncle who ate flies or something and wasn't permitted outside, a World War I gas victim, or an ex-All American who had taken to drink or exposing himself. Our evenings passed like ones in the tropics, my father snoozing on the sofa, as if under a mosquito net, my mother and aunt reading drowsily side by side in shimmers of heat. Once I donned bathing trunks, in December, because the house seemed to call for it. Inside a home, eccentricities were permitted. My mother and Aunt Milly were convinced that hordes of brilliant break-in artists, burglars, waited outside for the chance to pounce. They locked the front door, bolted it, and hooked the screen every night before retiring. They did a two-way job on the side door, and kept a permanent barricade on the back porch. In bed in darkness—my father now down at the depot working third trick because he preferred its silence and the way it left him alone—I could hear their ritualistic conversation float between their rooms. "Belle, did you bolt the front door?" my aunt would start.

"Now, Belle, why did you have to say that?" They both called each other Belle; neither knew why because it wasn't either one's name. "Why didn't you say something about it when we were both downstairs?"

"Well, I can't remember checking it."

"Now I've just got to go down and make sure. I could just shoot you."

"And check the side door while you're at it—and the back porch!"

Silence. Safe. Now we could all sleep without fear of armed assault. Through the decades not one burglar had ever shown. There was one or two scare stories—before my time—about someone who had knocked on the door sometime after dark but never a bona fide example of an actual thief. And the funny thing was, no attention was ever paid to windows. The doors could be padlocked, bolted, nailed down and then a window would be open a few feet away. When I mentioned the irony of this fact once to my aunt, she tried to comprehend but then gave up. She simply couldn't visualize anyone entering a house other than through the standard portals. Strange—but that was how it was at our house.

I saw Pancho's home as slightly criminal where the rule book was thrown away. You could strut in there any old time, not even bothering to knock. Through the heat of day and into warm evenings his Uncle Buford would be stationed on the front porch in a rocking chair, creaking ever so slightly back and forth. In the winter he moved inside along with the porch and lawn furniture. He did not make his living at one of the standard professions, but as a politician. He was sometimes grandly a senator in the state legislature, something that took about a week of his time each year, or he held a post in the county that went by a murky title—assessor of this, clerk of that. In every big election—for U.S. Senator, the governorship, the presidency—he seemed to have some sort of undercover hand. We always knew when an election was near by the number of long black cars parked in front of his house. And inside you might find really important men, people whose pictures had been in the newspaper and who made public speeches, chatting with old Uncle Buford in the corner. They seemed ashamed to be caught there—even by a fifteen-year-old boy—and would never run over to pump your hand as they did on the street around election time. The local newspaper called Uncle Buford a "boss," someone who could hand over votes. And once a man running for governor, on the opposition ticket, called Uncle Buford a "hatchet man." We loved that down at the poolroom, and from then on he was raised in our estimation. A hatchet man. Someone who fought mean and dirty and all-out *to win*. You could tell that Pancho, by the way he lowered his dark eyes and grinned, was proud of his uncle's new title.

Uncle Buford's door was never locked, even at night or when everyone was away. Every time I flew in, often four times a day, taking the stairs three at a time, I hoped against reason once again that I might catch Mary Sue—Uncle Buford's daughter, Pancho's cousin—in her bloomers. There was no way to describe her body other than to say it was a first-class ticket to the loony bin: Those hips and tits and the way her calf muscles swelled as she walked! Oh, God! One starry summer night the Sheik—someone else I could never remember not knowing, whose Lebanese father ran a restaurant—coaxed several of us to climb a tree by her bedroom window. He was tagged the "Sheik" because of his adoration of Maria

21

Montez in desert pictures; also the name paid tribute to Lebanese ancestors who, we liked to picture, were strong, burnoosed figures riding the sands.

Just climbing the tree, believing there was even a remote chance of seeing Mary Sue undress, caused my bone to rise against the bark. Out on branches we squirmed, Pancho excluded in deference to his kinship, leaning to peer under the half-closed yellow shade. Being able to see the texture of her bedspread, the odd, intimate touches of her well-worn teddy bear and her dresser's girlish shade of pink caused my heart to pump me back and forth. And then she whirled in, stood a second with her hands on those hips, thinking perhaps. Thinking to take off all her clothes? Please . . . yes. She pulled her light-blue sweater over the top of her dark head, causing the small gold basketball on a feather-thin chain to bounce on her slip. Her slip! Bra next . . . then *bloomers!* A thumb hooked under her slip strap, and then a strange jarring noise. The sickening sound of cracking wood. "Oh, shit, boys," the Sheik cried, "I'm going."

He fell the equivalent of two stories from his perch, all two hundred-and-some pounds of him down through leaves and bark and birds' nests, snapping limbs off like toothpicks along the way, landing flat out on his back in a muffled plop. Mary Sue raised the shade and looked out into our terror-struck eyes. Chillingly, with no embarrassment, as if she'd been prepared for this moment since the start of menstruation, she said, "All right, I see every one of you. That's Ghazi down on the ground, too. If I catch any of you boys doing this ever again I'm going to tell your mommas."

The Sheik was up on one knee when we swung to the ground, dazed but still in there. None of us worried about injury. All had been knocked senseless at football many times; some (myself) had taken a baseball at full speed between the eyes, a slung bat across the temple, or a flying fist to the jaw. You just saw stars and woke up the next day with bruises and blurred vision, that was all, nothing to get excited about. But *she* had seen *us*—so we'd better clear out. She'd even called the Sheik by his real given name—Ghazi—something that was the scariest note of all. "Listen, you guys," the Sheik said, in that staccato delivery he had, shaking his head like a fighter, "I'm going back up. Who's coming and who's chickenshit?"

"But we can't see nothing now, Sheik. Come on."

"Like hell. She'll really think she's safe after this, and then there's no telling what. I don't know about you guys but I've got to see me some of Mary Sue's snatch or I'm going crazy."

The Sheik pulled his weight again up the tree against great odds, taking a helping hand to the ass and foot when he could. He was without fear—for, you see, he had no momma.

He ate whole meals of French fries, pickles, and ice cream, never having to worry about regular dinners and washing your hands and brushing your teeth. He helped out at peculiar hours in his father's restaurant—the Roxy—helping himself also to cans of beer, cigarettes, and folding money for pool. He was an excellent and graceful shot, flicking the little finger of his cue-holding hand up just so before ramming the stick home. He had a superb eye, but he also had bad luck—as if he was cozier in defeat than victory. An opponent would "luck in" the winning ball after the Sheik had dazzled a crowd with racks of intricate banks and kisses and long-range slams. Wiped out chronically, he left no stone unturned for fresh funds. Once we palmed some books from my own home— *Goodbye, Mr. Chips* among them—and he sold them to the sweaty, bald secondhand dealer who did business in a dim light under an avalanche of yellowing print. "I can't go in there with you, Sheik," I had said, "because the man knows me. He'd tell my momma."

"You're scared, aren't you? You're afraid to go through with it."

"No, it's just common sense. I'll wait out on the corner."

"O.K., by God, I'll show you I'm not afraid."

He came out with his hand over the money in his pocket, tainted money that couldn't be treated in any ordinary way. Technically, since the books had come from my own home, I was entitled to half, but in a rush of camaraderie I suggested that the Sheik decide what to do with it. He went, without breaking stride, to the poolroom where he took on—in wreaths of talcum and the creak of chalk—the second best stick in town. Old Curly. And lost. In a little under an hour he lost it all. And the next week, in one of his daily treks in and out of my house, we both heard my mother make a startling announcement. "You know, Ghazi, I was down at Tad's Book Fair yesterday afternoon when I found a book that actually had come from here. Isn't that the oddest thing?"

"Yes, ma'am, I guess so."

"He said a young man, a *heavy-set* young man, had sold it to him. I'm just mystified as to who it might be."

"Yes, ma'am. Well, I just stopped by for a minute. I got to be running."

He left without his usual raid on the kitchen. He would eat anything, things that even animals turned up their noses at —cold gravy, jars of pickled cauliflower, day-old hard biscuits—anything within sight as he flew past shelves, the pots on the stove, and into the far depths of the refrigerator. My mother often offered him food, in addition, saying later, "Poor Ghazi, he was so little when his mother died."

In the vacant lot beside the house the Sheik grabbed me by my shirt collar and shook me. "She knows, she knows! I'm going to tell her that you were in on it, too. I'm not going to take the whole rap, Bones."

24

"Listen. She doesn't know for sure, I tell you. But if you confess, we're sunk. Don't be an idiot. She'll forget about it in a week or so. Believe me."

"I ought to knock the shit out of you."

"Why?"

"Because she found out about it, that's why."

Once at Ping-Pong at the Maple Street Pool the Sheik had broken his Ping-Pong ball on a hard slam. (We brought our own balls to the game and they cost ten cents each.) He demanded then that I give him mine. Why? I had wanted to know. Because, he explained angrily, it was just by chance that my ball hadn't been in use then. He shouldn't be made to suffer simply because of the fickleness of fate. How could you argue with that? And it was impossible to reason now with him, for he didn't live under the same code and logic the rest of us went by. He used to jack off under his coat in the movies, for instance. And for that reason you didn't exactly break your neck to go with him. Because just when Maria Montez came on in a desert picture or somebody like Gene Autry's girl friend showed up at the ranch, the Sheik started banging away as if in a convulsion, his eyes rolling and his jacket with our school colors jumping. Nearly any woman could do it to him although he had favorites you sort of prepared yourself for—Maria Montez leading the list. And sometimes in class —if a woman teacher was chalking something up on the blackboard, her butt twitching—there would come the report of old Sheik firing another one off from the back. He always took back seats so no one could catch him from behind. And during the action parts of our movies, the fistfights and horse chases, he would clutch at my arm: "Listen, Bones, if you ever squeal on me for jacking off I'm going to beat the shit out of you. Remember that."

The truth was that the Sheik could do it. Unlike most fat

boys he was extremely quick and dangerous when the occasion called for it. Around the start of our adolescence I had made the mistake of talking him into putting on the gloves with me and fighting before a crowd in the vacant lot. In childhood I had whipped him continually and I assumed that the strengths and weaknesses of that earlier, halcyon time would carry on forever. The red Sears and Roebuck gloves were sixteen ounces, and we had our chatty seconds lace them up. That was the high juicy moment, a scary one really, feeling the gloves go on and knowing you were committed to a fight. Someone went, "Bong!" and the Sheik marched straight across the cream-colored dust and knocked me a good ten yards against a tree. I didn't even see the punch coming.

From then on, knowing he could take me, he settled all arguments and even mild irritations by being ready to fight. Generally, though, he was funny and laughed at my own routines and was always one who would take that first step into some new strange facet of adulthood. You liked to be around a guy like that. But just to keep the record straight and up to date, he would hit me occasionally without benefit of gloves. Anytime I saw his fist double up I started talking a mile a minute. The shot could arrive like a bullet, over two hundred pounds of argument behind it, making me see stars for hours and feel aches for weeks. The Sheik was living proof that jacking off didn't make you weak. And he also had an excuse for being so cunt crazy, claiming to have actually seen a few and even—beautiful story—of having frigged to a frazzle a girl cousin on summer visits to South Carolina. Good old Sheik. Over and over I used to pry him into relating once more how he would slip into his girl cousin's room after lights out and do it. One version—my favorite—even had the girl initiating it all and teaching him how. God!

And the day after we had left him shinnying back up the

26

walnut tree, he informed us in the poolroom that he had seen Mary Sue's bare tits. Her titties! I knew he was lying, but I believed him anyhow. If you know what I mean. Anyhow, she changed her room shortly afterward to across the hall where no tree limbs waved. Girls were a total mystery.

I found Pancho one Saturday morning in his room smoking. Actually, he was going around batting the air to kill the evidence. The cigarette was hidden out of sight, held toward his palm by a pinch of his forefinger and thumb. Even alone he hid it. "Keep this quiet. Uncle Buford would kill me if he found out."

"Gimme one," I said.

"Asshole. You don't smoke. It's just wasted on you."

"Gimme one anyhow. Don't be so tight."

He was right about my not having the nicotine habit. Either you had it or you didn't—no halfway thing about it. It was like one of those science fiction stories where a whole town is taken over, one person at a time, by some bizarre otherworldly power. The people would be acting as normal as pie and then, almost casually, reveal some sort of telltale mark that showed they were doomed forever. In school before the first class some boy would come up to you and his breath would nearly knock you down with a new, sharp sting. You knew another smoker had been added. And from then on you would notice a rectangular bulge somewhere on his clothing, his teeth changing color, and those stains starting between his first two fingers. Nicotine fiends took shortcuts through alleys on their way to school, like a scout patrol, gray plumes jetting from their lips. And through the day they devised ways to suck in the medicine every hour or so; some favored the boiler room, others the lavatory or a quick trot out the gym in abbreviated wear. The only way to stay safe was never inhale, never once. I loved to bum a weed now and then, which was like scratching yourself every so often. But I felt no real need for it. I lit up, held the smoke in my mouth, and then pretended to inhale by drawing in through the nose. It was the swagger connected with smoking I enjoyed; therefore, my preference for Hav-A-Tampas, no inhaling required. Actually, a fake cigar from the dime store would have satisfied my needs just as long as I had the pretense of smoking. But Pancho was different. He went through the frills to the very heart. At age sixteen he inhaled so hard his jugular bulged and he had to have a pack and a half a day.

"Look, Pancho. You let me have a weed now and I'll turn over the library mail job to you next week."

"Promise?"

"Swear."

"A deal."

Going to the post office in the morning for school library mail was a prized assignment. I was selected by Miss Georgia Ann Kyker because, I suppose, I looked and acted studious —meaning quiet, someone to entrust with the U.S. mail. In truth, those times my face was serene I was having reveries of behinds in tight skirts and rounded breasts under cashmere. A trip outside the prison was enjoyable to me, but nothing I desperately craved. For a nicotine fiend it was his one chance in the day to light up in leisure and not under pressure.

I fiddled around with the cigarette Pancho gave me, making a big show of flicking ashes into my palm and then throwing them out the window. We never did feel forced to talk to each other, going for stretches in which we gazed at the floor or ceiling. Then we might suddenly fling out a *non sequitur* that seemed to have no rhyme nor reason. "You know, Bones, you can't shoot pool worth a shit. You choke."

"You're the luckiest son of a bitch that ever lived."

"The Sheik ate Uncle Buford's lunch the other day, I tell you? Made Uncle Buford mad as hell, and I got blamed. You got to watch the fat boy night and day."

"*There's a star speckled banana-er sticking somewhere . . .*" a burst of song, just because it felt good, lyrics, *de rigueur,* dirty.

"You can't sing worth a shit, Bones."

"You can't spell anything over one syllable."

"What's a silly belle?"

It was more comfortable being around Pancho than, say, the Sheik. The Sheik could never sit still and be reflective. And also, back in my mind, unarticulated, was the knowledge that I could beat the Sheik in the quest for girls, something that was going to matter most of all shortly. The Sheik was going to have a hard time of it, and would be no competition or help. But Pancho—with those black secretive eyes—was a match for me.

Her name was Meredith Lancaster, and from the moment I saw her face come suddenly around a corner at Mount Castle High School I knew this was It. Hadn't the songs and movies and novels by Charles Dickens made it Love at First Sight? God, I was prepared. She had indistinct freckles over a strong nose, large, soft, wide-spaced eyes, and a high forehead. Pretty; you'd love to be seen strolling down the street with her. She wore slightly scuffed saddle-oxfords and clean white socks neatly turned down. I drew my breath in sharply, as a portent of things to come.

"Which way is Miss Godsey's room?" she wanted to know, not looking at me, probably not even seeing me. Books were pressed against her chest. She was lost, the first day of class, a Transfer.

"It's there," pointing quickly. "Right over there."

As I watched her hair, a taffy color, bounce, I thought of ploys I might have used to be remembered, gags the fellows might have appreciated, like, "You can't miss Miss Godsey. She weighs a ton." And then like a flash into the lavatory to wet the old hair and push the little wave in near the part. And, when the coast was clear, dabbing some powder I kept secreted in a handkerchief on the latest pimple of the day. I wanted to have one more quick look at her and drink in everything I could, the way her shoe strings fell, the locker she used, the way she carried her books. Tangible items that could lend verisimilitude to daydreams.

I had already heard about her. She had gone before to the private school connected with the college on the outskirts of town, something called the Training School, a grassy, ivy-covered domain for those with a doctor or preacher or somesuch for a father. That kind of father strolled confidently into the Sanitary Barbershop every morning to have his shoes whipped to a high shine while lying back flat for his face to be steamed, scraped, patted, pulled, and finally bay rummed. Such confidence—as everyone glanced his way while he joked and passed on wisdom to the slack-jawed barber and the grinning shoeshine boy. The private school bunch—the sons and daughters—had their distinctions, too. See someone down on Main Street with braces on his teeth, and you knew his school. Those from the private school were more polite, got beat up more often (the boys), and wore cleaner clothes and faces than those of us in public school. Uncle Buford had placed Pancho and Mary Sue in the private school for a stretch when his political fortunes were running high, and then they transferred when insurgents whittled away his power base and he developed ailments. At times, I thought I found remnants of Pancho's tour on the other side, his abrupt finickyness from time to time for one thing—or what I took to be finickyness.

He went crazy if someone touched him accidentally in a movie.

In his room at Uncle Buford's, which reeked of athletic gear, I said, "What do you think of Meredith Lancaster?" trying for a casual tone, my voice feeling light.

"Oh, shit. Now don't tell me you've gone and fallen for that girl, Boney."

"Did I say that? I just asked what you thought of her, nothing about me being hooked. God almighty, I don't know a thing about her."

"Guys . . . fall for her. She gets what she wants."

"But she's a nice girl. You can tell that, can't you?"

"I've known Meredith since back in Training School. There's nothing I don't know about her. You think she's so special. Well, every other guy does, too. All the boys want her. She likes that."

"I don't want her. All I'm doing is asking you a few plain simple questions. Come on. Has any guy fooled around with her? Does she go with anybody now?"

"She's nice. It's just . . . will you forget about her, Boney?

I wanted only a few more facts to build dreams on. "Meredith has a brother, doesn't she? What's he like?"

"A dope, I think. He's in the army overseas. Some place in Italy."

"She probably thinks a lot of him."

"He's her brother."

"I like her older sister, Joan. Boy, she's the nicest thing. Sweet and real good-looking. Is Meredith like her?"

"Meredith is not as good looking. Got too big a nose. . . . Come on, let's kick some football."

In a side yard nearby, with thick green grass and wild onions, we stood at opposite ends and booted a hard scruffy ball to each other. Soon we were betting a nickel on who could kick it further. I had grown a foot in the last year with no gain in weight, in one of nature's great feats of humor, while Pancho had been presented with a battery of bulging muscles and large veins straining out. I had obeyed all laws for clean living, including the brushing of the teeth four times a day, while Pancho had smoked and kept late hours and now, in the unfairness of it all, beat me. And since this was an unmistakable contest, everything boiled down to a game, he was unrelenting in that way he had—almost crazy, black eyes darting and ablaze, wanting to go on and on, till I was beaten and beaten and there was no doubt about it.

"Boney, I'll give you a chance to get your money back. Let's play two-man football, ten cents on a touchdown."

With a sidewalk as one goal line and a clothesline as another, we ran at each other, four tries at scoring before the ball changed hands. A couple of elbows into my chest, a foot stepping on my head, and I gave up. He took all my money, became convinced that I couldn't be talked into running home for more, and then relaxed. We lay back on the grass, breathing deeply, blades of grass between our teeth.

"Boney, you let me shake you off. You just couldn't hold on."

"You son of a bitch, you elbowed me. Played dirty."

"I know," he said, chortling.

A feeling of camaraderie; good buddies once more. "Say, does Meredith live on a farm or something?"

"You bastard, you know perfectly well she don't. She lives out around the Pine Crest Addition. You have to have a car to get out there."

"Yeah? What's her home look like?"

"It's stucco and white. And it's got some brick in it, I think."

"Big?"

"Yeah. I don't know. Why don't you go out and take a look for yourself? Or ask her."

We had no car at our home, the bane of my life, dependent upon the aegis of the Yellow Cab Company for emergencies. The Sheik often stole his father's car and I could get him to drive me, but it was never a leisurely, eye-filling ride with the Sheik. He was, surprisingly, too good a driver, and had to constantly demonstrate his ability. He skidded off in first, took second with his little finger extending from the gearshift as if holding a teacup, and then down smartly into third while he shot around trucks and cars and cut in a blur around corners. His driving was like his pool shooting, fantastically graceful. And his form was so good that it became everything, doing away with any scenery watching. He was like those novelists and film-makers, encountered in later life, whose technique was so good you forgot what they were saying. It was Pancho himself who eventually drove me past Meredith Lancaster's home.

It was around midnight, I had already had my first wet dream of the evening, and I was startled bolt upright by honking on the street. My second-story room faced the street, and I stuck my head out the window. Uncle Buford's green, 1940 V-8 Ford was rumbling out there, Pancho behind the wheel. "Come on, Boney. I ain't got all night."

"Everybody's in bed. How can I come out?"

"Come on. We'll only be gone a few minutes. I may not have the chance at a car again for some time."

The moment I had heard the horn, I knew I was going. But I had to be coaxed for just a little while; and I could count on Pancho to coax. Into my clothes in a flash, with presence of mind to change my wet-dream shorts, and then down the hall, explaining to my awakened mother, "It's Pancho, Mom. Something's up. I'll only be out a little while."

"Be sure to lock after you."

"And bolt and latch when you come back," my aunt called from the opposite room.

In the vibrating Ford Pancho wore a T-shirt, khakis without a belt, and no shoes. Uncle Buford had roused him from bed himself to drive out for cigarettes—such a wonderful command for a guardian to make. We were now detouring from the cigarette run, going on a joy ride, trying for a taste of adulthood. Pancho carefully shifted, frowning, as if he had the controls of a B-32. We rolled beneath lush tree branches, past darkened homes, the Ford's panel lights alive and glowing in front of us. We had mobility, could go anywhere, were wheeling a car. We were doing what the big folk did! "I smell something," Pancho said, stopping, nostrils flaring. "Do you smell rubber burning? Smell carefully."

"I don't smell a thing."

"Rubber!"

He tested the hand brake, got out and smelled the motor and all four tires, and then drove on satisfied for the moment we weren't on fire. A little past the Pine Crest Addition, seeming to know where he was going, not choosing the path at random, he cut onto a small lane through an arched brick column as if we might be entering a private estate. The headlights washed over a sign and I strained my eyes: "Drive Carefully. Our Children May Be at Play!" My own home was on a street that served as part of a veritable national highway, and once a small girl from down the block had not gotten out of the way fast enough and had had her head crushed like a pumpkin by a trailer-truck. After the funeral, her father, a man in overalls, went back to rocking on his front porch, watching the traffic hurl past as before, uncomplaining. On this quiet, narrow lane Pancho slowed before a large white,

stucco-and-brick home. No light shone, but the moon illumi-
nated shadowy lawn and porch furniture. On the second story
the blinds were up halfway, some of the windows open. "This
is where she lives," Pancho said.

"Yeah? Wonder which room she sleeps in?"

"Probably she took the best one, knowing her."

"Yeah, she's probably in the best one."

"Well, got your eyes filled, Boney? Or do you want to
camp out here all night and watch her go to school in the
morning?"

"I don't care about her, for crying out loud! I just wanted
to know a few things about her because she was new at
school. That's all!"

On the drive back he thought he smelled burning rubber a
couple of more times, and in my own old room I closed my
eyes and saw again those darkened, second-story rooms with
the blinds half-up.

We were never formally introduced—unthinkable in that
loose, beehive world of school: "Meredith, I'd like for you to
meet Boney. Boney, Meredith." We met by having a class or
two together, going in the same direction down the hall a few
times, and standing near one another in the noon cafeteria
line. Ernie Peoples, a redhead who fingerwaved his hair, gre-
garious, possessor of a learner's driving permit at age fourteen
—voted to have Best School Spirit—squealed on me, by his
own admission, to Meredith. Old Ernie. He had no nickname,
probably because he played no sports and didn't hang around
the poolroom, but he had a distinction in my book. He swore
he was screwing a flaxen-haired, thirteen-year-old girl in the
basement of his apartment house, and wanted me to hide behind the furnace and watch him do it. I was always missing

the times, though, and kicking myself—their having just finished or her not being in the mood. Ernie stopped Meredith walking out of school one day, and said, "Guess who's interested in you?"

"Who?" He told her. "You're kidding. Oh, no. He never says a word to me. He can't be."

When Ernie told me the dialogue, I felt my heart sink yet I couldn't be angry. He must know what he was doing, else how could he screw in his basement and drive his family car since age fourteen. "How did she look when you told her?"

"Those big eyes got bigger, and she pulled her books high up on her chest. She's the cutest old thing, I just love her." Ernie had spent earlier years in Alabama and had a more Deep South quality about him than those of us strictly from the mountains. "You're never going to get yourself any cause she's too nice. But why don't you go with her? Or try to, boy."

She would be squatting, skirt tucked in severely, getting books out of the bottom of her locker—and I would hurry past. She sat on the other side of the room in geometry class, and I would flick my eyes her way, drinking in her profile, relishing the open book before her, the polished wood that held her. ". . . And now I'm going to have someone come up here and finally work out this problem on the blackboard," Mr. DePew, a wisp of a teacher who could get surprisingly tough, said from the front. "I'm tired of fooling around with people who are asleep. All right! Come up here, Johnny, and give us the square of the hypotenuse. I can see he's awake."

"I'm sorry, Mr. DePew, I wasn't following what you were saying. What was that?" *I was following my darling Meredith!*

It got a laugh, Mr. DePew went crimson, and Meredith turned in a beautiful smile. Any attention from her was better than none. To be noticed, just to be noticed. My conversations, face-on with her, would never do the trick. I could only manage one or two strangled words from a set format I'd memorized before blushing to my fingertips and wishing I was dead. The telephone would have to be used. I had often seen my revered older brother—now away in the navy—nonchalantly take the upright black instrument, used mostly for grocery and coal orders, out the side door, slamming the door on the cord, and then talk while hunched up on the rickety side steps.

I paced the backyard, throwing gravel at the barn, picturing her fine home and the pretty way she would look breathing into a phone. Go ahead. *Faint heart ne'er won fair lady!* (Eleventh grade, Miss Godsey's English class, *Don Quixote*.) When I count to twelve, I told myself angrily, we're going to pick up that phone and we're going to call 960. What are you, goddamnit, a man or a mouse? *Faint heart ne'er won fair lady!* All day, through every class, stealing glimpses of her whenever I could, I daydreamed about this call. Was it going to end with me turning chicken? That wasn't what I'd been taught. *A winner never quits, and a quitter never wins!* (Seventh grade. Midget football. Coach Travis.)

"Supper!" my mother called from inside the house. "Everyone wash his hands. Johnny! Belle!"

I strode to the phone, picked it up without thinking, heard the country-girl operator's immediate whine: "Number, please?"

"Nine-six-o," I said, in a rush, feeling my heart nearly coming out my ears. It rang, it actually rang.

"Hello," a brisk, older woman. Probably her mom.

"Meredith. Is Meredith there?"

"Just a minute," in a kind of singsong. A long pause, in which I watched cars go by on the street, a scratch on my hand received in a basketball game—all seeming unreal and hard to comprehend. If someone had hit me on the head, I still couldn't have dropped that receiver. I could hear her picking up the instrument on the other end.

"Hello."

"Meredith? This you, Meredith? Meredith."

"Yes."

"How's the weather out your way?"

"Who's this?"

"Bones."

"Who?"

"John. Johnny. From school. Think the rain is going to be good for the rhubarb?" My debonair wit must be slaying her. I could hear her laughing. "I thought maybe someday, you know, we could go to a movie together. I don't have wheels at the moment, something a little unfortunate in that department at present," making a picture in my own mind of a family car in the repair shop or a learner's permit revoked. "But how would you like to double-date?"

"I can only go out on Friday nights. And I have to be in by eleven."

"Well, uh . . ."

"We could always go someday after school. If something's on you really want to see."

"Van Johnson's on in *Thirty Seconds Over Tokyo* Monday /Tuesday at the Majestic. It's a war picture. It should be good."

"Oh, that sounds just fine. Why don't we go then Tuesday? If that's all right with you."

"Fine, yeah, swell. I'll see you in school and we'll make all the arrangements. And, Meredith?"

"Yes?"

"Don't take any wooden nickels."

A laugh. A date, a real date. Boy!

We met at the top of the long concrete steps after the last class on Tuesday, nodded, and began the journey. It pleased me to watch classmates glance our way—watch them look, now that I'm with Meredith!—and I put a little swagger into my stride. She carried her books, as usual, high up against her chest. Even though I should have been taking some home for study, my hands were free. I wanted to get at any required pocket change in a hurry. At the candy and popcorn counter inside the theater, I waved grandly. "Choose whatever you like. The sky's the limit."

"Oh, could we get some popcorn? I'd just love some."

To have ourselves occupied in rifling pellets into our mouths relieved me of worrying about taking her hand. It would be so dramatic, suddenly holding a definite, intimate part of her, that it caused a catch in my breath to picture it. Yet weren't most guys taking girls' hands throughout the length and breadth of the Majestic? I was letting down the system. On screen Van Johnson, freckle-faced and in a flier's uniform, was having a romantic scene himself with Phyllis Thaxter, someone who resembled Meredith a bit, I thought. The actress had the same healthy good looks, the same aura of niceness, a remoteness that kept you intrigued but wouldn't let you get close enough to spoil things. If she and old Van ever did it, it would have to be done in a welter of smiles and good humor, with no sweat, nothing like the fuck books had it. Van Johnson, grinning a little, cupped Phyllis Thaxter's beaming face in his hands; they looked intently at each other. Love. "Tell me. How come you're so cute?" He was going off to bomb Tokyo with Spencer Tracy and the other guys.

Our knees, in keeping with tradition, were propped against the seats in front and we rested as far down as our spines would allow. At least I knew how to do that. The last ball of popcorn shot and the empty box scooted beneath the seat, a gnawing thirst for water ballooning, I saw in the pale light that Meredith's slim white hand was there over the arm-rest. Could she actually be ready—inviting my hand to take hers? Now I see the bombs wiggling down on Tokyo, bad guys and buildings flying sky-high, and I command my hand to go into action. It starts, gets nearly there, and then, in a total breakdown of control and nerve, returns to scratch my head, pull my nose, and rub beneath my chin, like a pet returning home. I'm doing a lot of nonchalant yawning, too. And then the chance passes; she moves her hand to her knee. Never in a million years could I do any work around her knees. I can relax again now.

Outside we moved into late afternoon sunshine, into what looked like the last moments of our "date." What was I supposed to do now? "Would you like to catch a Coke or soda or something?"

"No, thanks. They're expecting me home now."

"Will you take a rain check then?"

"Oh, yes. Sure," smiling.

I was still being suave, throwing in the wit. We walked along, she hurrying us just a little, going up Thompson Street that led into the highway out of town. I didn't know where we were going. "Could I put you into a taxi?"

"Oh, no, that's all right."

"Well, how are you going to get home? Going to take the bus?"

"Don't worry. I'll get there," talking quietly, shifting the books higher on her chest.

We came then to the crossroads. My home was a couple of blocks to the left. Hers was a long way off to the right. We faced each other, and again I didn't know what to do with my hands. They were swinging up and down. "Sure you don't want me to walk with you to your home?"

"No, you'd just have to walk all the way back yourself."

"Well."

"Thanks so much for taking me to the movie. I loved it. It was so good."

"That's O.K. And, Meredith," throwing out a Van Johnson grin, hearing myself actually say, "how come you're so cute?"

She smiled, ducking her head, wheeled, and took off toward the horizon. Though I hated myself, I stole a glance at her calves. They looked firm and strong, her white socks whipping back and forth in a fast stride. A real "date" accomplished, I'd done it! Tingling and in a daze, I was nearing home when I heard my name called. Pancho jumped out from behind a tree in the vacant lot. "Hey, Boney, how was the date?"

"How did you know about it?"

"I saw you leave her up on the corner. You were so blind you didn't see me across the street. I was waving like crazy. Goddamn, you just left her up there like that? To walk all the way home?"

"Well, she said she wanted to."

"Boney, you are something, I swear. It's five miles to her house! You drove with me that night, remember?"

"She said she wanted to, I tell you."

"Boney, Boney. Don't you know you can't always believe what a girl first tells you. The Long Walk. You sure you didn't see the *Bataan Death March* down at the Majestic and get inspired?"

"Awwww . . ."

The screen door snapped as usual, the standard smell of corn bread came from the kitchen, and the late afternoon sun creased the stairs in that certain way. But I had an altogether new feeling now—racing toward my room—of being half off the high-diving board at the Maple Street Pool in a crazed, compulsive leap and not knowing how I was going to touch the water.

Two

In my room I plugged in the phonograph with the steel needle I had bought with savings from a paper route, one of the many jobs I had hung onto for awhile. I had worked a year at that route, six days in the afternoon, up before daybreak and freezing on Sunday, and somehow had managed to make fifteen dollars. At times it seemed I was losing money, daydreaming while chugging along on my silver-fendered bike, forgetting to collect from some customers, trying mistakingly and to my regret to collect twice from others. My one dream was that I would one day catch the lady of the house in her bloomers. I must have been the only paper-route boy in America to never surprise anyone in his underwear. Once a woman, who smoked Wings and had a nervous Pekingese, wore shorts, but that was the closest I ever came.

The paper route was a journey many of us went through. The first days were nervous, but exciting: the smell of fresh print, seeing the large wedge of papers shrink to a few as the route went along, the relief of homeward peddling at the end. A few customers tried to gyp you; older, more experienced boys warned you that Mrs. So-and-so would say she'd paid when she hadn't and that Mr. Something-or-other was hard to corner at collection time. I followed all such advice devotedly, and then forgot or couldn't keep my own books in order. My only income seemed to come from selling "extras" to people along the way. On Sundays I had more "extras" than usual and steady buyers who came groggily to front doors in bathrobes or who left dimes under doormats or in mailboxes. My paper was not the hometown one, which had routes more sought after, but the Knoxville *News-Sentinel*. Pedaling down gray streets on Sunday morning, I screamed, *"KnoxVILLLLE Newwwwwwwws-Sentinel!"* Occasionally a fist would shake from an open window and a, "You out there, paper boy, be quiet!" But enough could crawl to doors to make my screaming worthwhile. My last stop was a house on a hill that had an apple tree out front, a tableau that was usually bathed in rich Sunday sunshine by the time I pedaled there. The dime— sometimes mysteriously two—would be under a brick on the front porch. I never saw who lived there and neither had the boy who had preceded me, a fellow with a badly sewn-up harelip. Sometimes there would be a note along with the coin: "Help yourself to the apples, and take some home for your momma to cook in a pie if you like." Those apples—route completed, pockets full of dimes, and juice running down my chin—tasted as good as any apples ever would. . . .

To go with the heavy portable phonograph I had enough

money left to buy only two records: "The Blue Danube" and the "Vienna Waltz" rendered by Harry Horlick and orchestra on one platter, Al Jolson singing "Sewanee" and "Mammy" on the other. When I toted the package in, savings shot, my father immediately hit the ceiling. He said that one day, when there was an emergency, I'd realize the importance of *savings*. But I could never quite picture the magnitude of an emergency that would ever satisfy him. Possibly an emergency burial after death would do it; surely nothing in life would ever come up to his standards and money salted away would have to follow one to the grave. For if needing a car and wanting to hear music weren't high emergencies—what were? I couldn't swing a car on my savings, but I could a machine that made music. My father tried to return it like a shot, saying, "They'll palm off anything on an unsuspecting kid." But, to my overwhelming relief, was not successful—or he could have only pretended to have tried a return to teach me a lesson; he did things like that sometimes. The phonograph became a fixture in my room, using steel needles by the dozen and causing all minds within earshot to grow woozy with the lilt of old Vienna and the rhythm of Al Jolson.

After my "date" with Meredith, I thought the strings of Harry Horlick might be in order. The shade down tight—to preclude Pancho or the Sheik from catching me—I played "The Blue Danube" and the "Vienna Waltz" over and over, gliding about and pretending I was leading Meredith Lancaster in an evening dress with hooped skirt, myself, of course, in tails. Round and round I went, my heart pierced at times by the fear that she might still be trudging toward home. Maybe she would stop in one of those drowsy little grocery stores along the way, call her mother and have her come pick her up. She must know what she was doing. What did Pancho know? Round and round—a second fear overlapping the first and that was that now I was going to have to get a second "date." How? And what would we do?

It was no good imagining double-dating with Pancho—that is, if he could even get Uncle Buford's car for the occasion. He was into teasing girls and making them mad now, not using his potential at all. And he didn't appear as crazed about them as some of us did. No one would ever accuse the Sheik of lacking interest, but he was definitely out of the picture. Once we had double-dated the two Betsys together. They were close girlfriends, both named Betsy, both blossoming the same summer with apple-sized breasts and a fund of dirty jokes. They hung around the Chocolate Bar, a dim after-school hangout with a jukebox that played Glenn Miller, a pinball machine binging and zinging over the low notes. They smoked, one Betsy able to suck smoke to her gut and talk around a jiggling butt in her mouth. After we'd made the date for Friday night at seven sharp, the Sheik cornered me in the hall between classes, eyes delirious. "Boney, those girls fuck. Now don't they?"

"Sure, Sheik." I was depending upon his car; more technically, his father's car. "I wouldn't be a bit surprised at all."

"Why, you know goddamnit they do. The way that Betsy Price inhales. Now you're not standing there telling me girls that tell those kinds of jokes don't put out. Boney, we're going to get ourselves some pussy. Ain't we?"

"I bet we do."

Into civics class where we were taught about the high plateau on which our government was run; down to physics to learn eighteenth- and nineteenth-century principles by rote. In history, learning once more that Rome fell in A.D. 476, I felt a folded note slide onto my desk and under my hand: "Thay'll playe weith our peters if nothing else I bet!" From the back row the Sheik was waving and grinning away.

That Friday, late in the afternoon, we learned that the Sheik could not get the family car. His nuisance of a younger sister, Leila, had laid prior claim to it. What use could a girl have for a car anyhow? In times past she had always given in to every whim the Sheik might have, taking his shifts at the Roxy without complaint, loaning (giving) him money in a pinch, making telephone calls for him like an appointments secretary. Somehow she had seemed to get the Sheik mixed up with some strange, God-like figure. It was hard to comprehend. And now, stranger still, she couldn't be cajoled or threatened into waiving her rights for the car this night—even when the Sheik drew back his fist on her. She said she had promised to take some people to a church function. *Church?* It was the one area that took precedence over the Sheik's whims, and the infuriating thing to the Sheik was that she was a convert. "If they had a mosque here, by God, it'd all be different!" The father, Mr. Mansur, backed up Leila—as we knew he would. So we were shamed into calling the two Betsys—myself on the mouthpiece, the Sheik over my shoulder—telling them we must "walk 'em" tonight.

At the screen door of a one-story bungalow, situated on the hill above Main Street—the home of one of the Betsys (her father dead or missing, her mother out to the wee hours) —the Sheik and I appeared at seven on the dot. Freshly bathed, in starched white shirts with ties, shoes shined. The girls came out in a blossom of perfume, mouths blood-red with lipstick, faces ghostly with powder. They both wore identical types of loafers, pennies tucked in slots on top of each shoe. "Let's shove for the show," one said. "We can come back later and do some dancing. Music should be on WCHL by then. They got an old ball game on now."

We picked a Betsy at random and started off down the hill, the Sheik in the lead. He didn't hold her hand, didn't talk, didn't even look her way. When he had something to say—generally a bad witticism—he looked over his shoulder and said it to me. We sat through an Esther Williams swim movie, and then marched them back up the hill to the bungalow. Inside, the lighting put on low by one dim lamp in the corner, the girls sat down at each end of the sofa, as if inviting us to take seats beside them. The Sheik, instead, found the refrigerator and helped himself to meat from a leftover stew. I just couldn't sit down there by myself.

Into a silence, broken by stealthy chewing and refrigerator noises from the kitchen, the Betsy who could inhale to her gut began talking about boys—those a few grades ahead of us. How did she know boys that old? And she talked about them with such disdain, how they drank beer, crashed parties, and were so stuck-up. "But they can really jitterbug. And that's what gets them a lot of girls. It doesn't cut any ice with me, though."

"Me, either," the quieter Betsy said.

The Sheik returned, wiping his hands on a neatly folded handkerchief. Leila must have ironed it for him, someone instructing him to use it around girls, not licking his fingers or wiping his hands on the seat of his pants the way he did around the guys. "That Esther Williams sure can swim," he blasted suddenly, into the vacuum.

"I just loved her swimsuits tonight," a Betsy said. "They're so darling."

"Aren't they now," the other said. "Made out of that new latex. I just can't stand wearing my old wool one now."

"I can't stand the word *darling*," the Sheik said. "Everything *darling*. Darling this, darling that."

"What I can't stand," the Betsy who had used it said, "is the word *neat*. Those boys in the twelve-B say everything is

50

neat. Neat, neat, neat. One came up to me in the gym and said, 'You're real neat.' Ugggh, I can't stand it."

"Who was it?" the other Betsy said.

"Buddy Young."

"Ohhhhh!"

"You all heard the one about the Old Log Inn?" I said. The one joke I knew that always got a laugh had been playing around the edge of my brain since the evening began, ready to spring.

"You mean about the guy comes up to this parked car on a country road, sticks his head in and says, 'How far's the Old Log Inn?' and some guy gets out and beats him up? Yeah," said the Betsy who inhaled, "they were telling it down at the Chocolate Bar last week."

The other Betsy found raspy dance music on the radio, and everyone sat mute for awhile, eyes roving the ceiling and flicking at corners. "That stuff's too fast," the Sheik said. "Don't they ever play slow ones?"

"They play one every third time. But I feel like jitterbugging. Come on, somebody, let's dance. Neither one of you boys? O.K., Betsy, let's show 'em how." The inhaling Betsy had a cigarette going, dangling now from the corner of her mouth as she spun the other one in and out like a Yo-Yo. While the Sheik and I scooted further down in our seats, they tried out fancy little steps and new turns on each other. "Can you do this skip? Like this, on the beat. The boys in the twelve-B are all doing it."

"I'm going," the Sheik said, during a commercial for cattle feed. I had to follow because that's what you did on a double date. But I sort of liked watching the girls dance.

"Won't you boys stay and have a Nehi first? There's plenty in the icebox and they're just going to waste."

"No," the Sheik said, angry and gruff, in that sudden way he had. What did he have to be angry about now? When he grabbed me by the shirt, outside under the streetlight, I found out. "You said those girls would put out! Why didn't they fuck us?"

"I don't know." I was just as ignorant—perhaps more ignorant—than he was about how copulation was actually consummated. At least he had that yarn about his girl-cousin. I didn't even have a yarn. I knew that Rome had fallen in A.D. 476, but I didn't know the first thing about the phenomenon that was inflaming our minds twenty-four hours a day. I'd probably have to go to France to learn how.

"Boney, if you ever get me out on a wild-goose chase again, I swear I'm going to deck you good."

"Lord, Ghazi." Now was the time to use his given name. "Maybe we should learn how to jitterbug."

"That's for sissies. Besides I'd sweat like a hog, and they'd see it. Goddamnit, Boney," he said, releasing me, his anger evaporating as I knew it would if I waited long enough. "Let's go down to the Buffalo and run off a few."

Our hated ties yanked off and crammed in our hip pockets, shirts unbuttoned to mid-chest, we strutted in the poolroom—everyone knowing from our cleanliness that we'd been out on "dates." How great it felt being back in a familiar setting, where you could joke and laugh about real things, not make things up and feel on edge. The ritual we sprang into—grabbing cues, sprinkling powder on our hands, yelling for the rack boy—was like a warm bath at the end of a work day. Everything was now back where it belonged, unchanged. "Hey, Sheik, how's your hammer hanging?"

"Loose."

"Bones, you getting any?"

"A little on the radio."

The Sheik was certainly my buddy—but I couldn't bring him on a double date with Meredith. I'd have to pair up with someone who knew the ropes, someone suave. Waltzing around to "The Blue Danube," I knew who it called for.

It was Ernie Peoples who came through, enthusiastically. Decked out in a crimson polka-dot tie, wavy red hair steaming with Vitalis, he unfolded like a hothouse plant at the front door. He gabbed with my folks and aunt in the old high-ceilinged living room that Friday night while I made my final run before the bathroom mirror, patting on my cheeks some perfumed lotion that had come to the shelf as a bygone Christmas gift for someone. Ernie did not mind talking to grownups as much as some of us did; he always had a joke and easy banter handy, part of the charm he had acquired, I thought, from those early years in Alabama. He was laughing at the way my father was cracking a walnut when I came out of the bathroom. It made me a little sore to see him amused and enthralled over that, but my father was cracking them in some crazy way he had that no one else on earth ever employed, wielding a hammer with the nut stationed between two books. To make it worse, he was laughing right along with Ernie. But I had to be nice to Ernie because he possessed that miracle of all miracles: a car on Friday night.

Outside, easing away in his father's freshly polished black Dodge, both of us faint from the closed-in aroma of oils, perfume, powder, and dry cleaning, he said, "Now I want to see you kid around with old Meredith tonight. They love it," lowering his voice intimately, shifting gears, "the boys who know how to kid and what to do. Say, 'Hiya, good lookin', what's cookin'?' "

"Just like that? When I first go in her house?"

"Don't be afraid. I've seen you on that football field and down at the poolroom. You can do it, buddy."

"She has to be in by eleven. She told me."

"What'a ya mean, the show don't let out till ten, and then we'll have to catch a shake and bar-be-cues. That won't leave much time for smooching. And, boy, can that Sally Jane I got kiss. She has lips like balloons."

He pulled up smartly before the big stucco-and-brick home, motor idling, and I was on my own. Her mother came to the door, a woman with flecks of gray in her hair who resembled Meredith a little. She was dressed as if she might be going out that night, too. Once inside, everything was not so awesome. The cover for the couch showed some use, and *Time* was lying open on it as if a human being might have been reading it. The lighting came from lamps, just like in my house. But there were much fewer books here than in my own home; in fact, all I could see here was a shelf of what looked like unused *Encyclopaedia Britannica*. And just as I was relaxing, feeling I might have the slightest of chances, a tall, florid-faced man in golfing attire strode in and nearly shook my arm out of its socket. This was her father, no one about to crack nuts between two books with a hammer. He explained that he had just got in from the "course" where, doggone it, chuckling, Dr. Lovelace had just shot a hole in one. It shocked me that Dr. Lovelace—our minister at the Baptist church, who seemed to be against everything—should even be playing golf, let alone do something spectacular in it. Meredith's father called him *Tommy* Lovelace, too, not *Dr.* Lovelace the way everyone else I knew did. A few more words on golf, a comment or two on the threat of Communism, and he said, "Who are you?"

I told him, waited while he confused me with another

family in town, and then explained that my father had moved us to this town when I was three years old. He probably didn't know him; he was the telegrapher down at the depot. He kept nodding, holding his chin in his hand, legs crossed. It didn't take long to exhaust that subject, and Meredith still hadn't descended from above. "How you boys at Mount Castle going to do next fall?" he said.

He didn't have to say at what. I told him that the football team was rebuilding, but that we might win a few games. "You have to have a desire to win," he said. "And good coaching."

Meredith came down the steps swiftly, breathing, "Bye," here, "Sorry I'm late," there. God, girls. And then out the door, on waves of instruction, into the dark familiarity of Ernie's car. We all sat in the front seat, Meredith in the middle, our legs and hipbones touching with the swaying of the car. At Sally Jane's home, which was two-story and frame as mine was, Ernie popped out, slamming the door, and took off for the front door at a trot as if he knew exactly what he was doing. "Maybe we better get in the back so Sally Jane can sit with Ernie."

It was hard for me to see what Ernie ever saw in Sally Jane. I had known her forever, someone with the same kind of eyes as my own: the deep-set, southern kind that turned into slits when you laughed. It didn't matter that her chest had suddenly sprouted about the biggest pair in the junior class; it made no difference that those lips that used to be chronically chapped in the third grade had now, with the aid of lipstick, developed into soft inviting balloons. Had Ernie gone nuts? She came from the same kind of home we did—churchgoing a must, meals served religiously on time, a hard-working dad, lights out at eleven. Going after her was not moving one inch from the familiar, and romance had to be played on a more extraordinary field than that. Else what were all the movies and books and radio serials about?

Through the shifting shadows of the Majestic that night I kept an eye peeled for any snuggling-up from Ernie. If he took Sally Jane's hand in any recognizable grip or eased an arm down around her shoulder, then I would have to make contact with Meredith. That was how the game was played; we just understood it. Ernie could not take the knocks of football or dribble basketball or run a rack of pool, but he had me in being able to wheel a shiny black Dodge. And the fact that he was putting the meat to the thirteen-year-old in his apartment's furnace room on odd occasions—with so much minute, tantalizing detail you had to believe him—made him someone to reckon with.

But Ernie was busy making jokes, reaching over Sally Jane to poke me at punch lines—and I didn't discourage him, getting one back at him when my brain could work. The newsreel showed GI's, rifles at sling arms as we'd been taught in R.O.T.C., battening down a pontoon bridge while a heavy gale whipped and unsteadied them. "They better watch out," leaning over Sally Jane, giving us both a fine whiff of Juicy Fruit, "or they're gonna get their britches wet, Lord a mercy!"

"The fat one there may sink it, too. It looks like the Sheik."

"My brother's fighting over there," Meredith said quietly.

Of course! Dumbbell! How could I have forgotten? Image then of her in a spotless kitchen, placing oatmeal cookies in an overseas package; she would be wearing her saddle-oxfords, plaid skirt, and fluffy sweater. How could I have been so vile as to make a joke out of the terrain where such a noble and fortunate brother was fighting? Back in the car Ernie drove down Main to the Spot Drive-In, circling it once before settling in to see who was there and to be seen. Right before my shake and bar-be-cue pork was passed to me—all eyes glued to the incoming food—I swallowed my chewing gum. I couldn't bear the intimacy of spitting it out in my hand the regular way in front of Meredith. Where could I have put it? Ernie kept babbling like a cricket, sandwich juice running down his chin, swigging his shake. He had words for everyone—about Sally Jane's constant churchgoing, Meredith needing to be in by eleven, my hanging out in the poolroom. I sort of liked being identified with the old hangout in front of Meredith, letting her know I could take care of myself in the roughest setup there was. "Thank you ever so much there," he gushed to the little-girl curb-hop, in his Alabama accent, sliding an extra dime her way. "We know they don't pay you much here."

On the drive back his babbling stopped—as the rules called for it to do. Time was running out; moves must be made. One moment his hands were on the wheel, his back hunched forward, the next he had collared Sally Jane and moved her over next to him. When gears had to change, he let Sally Jane shift—barking, *"Now.* Throw it up. O.K., bring her down."

Meredith sat mute as a mummy against the door on her side, hands folded on her lap, staring straight ahead. All right, Bones, when we count to ten, you are to reach over and get something started. One, two . . . God, she's angry because of the necking going on up front. She's a nice girl, and you have to be extra careful. When we come to the grocery store before the turnoff to Sally Jane's house, you can then touch something. The car moved slowly but inevitably, and somewhere near the grocery store—where I remembered the ease and joy of buying Tootsie Rolls on the way to school—she said, "Does anyone know the time?"

"I can't take my hand off the wheel," Ernie said. "Look at it, Sally Jane, and tell her."

"Fifteen . . . I've got to get closer; pardon me, for squashing you, Ernie . . ."

"Ummmm."

"Fifteen till eleven."

Past the grocery store—chance lost—then two turns, and Ernie pulled up by Sally Jane's house where a porch light blazed. With no warning, no signal that I could see, Ernie whirled and flew into a deep soul kiss. Sally Jane's head didn't move, nearly out of sight, resting back against the seat as if this type of moment should never be advertised. Ernie, though, could be plainly seen, his Vitalis-lacquered waves glowing in the porch light, his eyes shut, moving from side to side as if drilling. Then it stopped, as though it hadn't happened, and he marched around to take Sally Jane to the door. I could see him kissing her again on the front porch, right under the naked light. How could you top a guy like that?

"Do you have any chewing gum?" Meredith said.

"Maybe I have some. Yes, here, take a whole stick."

"No, just let me tear this in two. I can't chew a whole one."

"Well, save the other half for later."

"No, I couldn't do that. You keep it."

She didn't make a move for the front seat when Ernie returned so we drove off as if being chauffeured. In fact, I said, "Home, James." Getting a mild chuckle. Every so often I spotted Ernie's eyes in the rearview mirror, checking up. I scooted a little closer to Meredith, pretending I was just stretching. And as the car weaved and bounced, taking to the high country road, I started around in a daze to get near her lips and then—having to look at her finally, feeling the ridiculousness of even considering myself worthy—I began a yawn that almost turned into a scream. Parked before her house, she said, "Well."

"Uh."

"I had the nicest time tonight. Thank you ever so much, Johnny. No, you don't have to walk me to the door. I'll just run in."

And she was gone, all moments lost, swallowed up again by the large stucco-and-brick home. For a few hours our fate had been the same: If a Jap bomb had fallen on the Majestic, we'd both be dead; or if in a car wreck, we'd have taken our lumps together. And during those brief magical hours we had been part of the same experience: me dating, she being dated. Now I was back in familiar territory, slouched down in the front seat, my knees against the dashboard. "How much sugar you get tonight?" Ernie asked.

"Awww."

"Buddy, I don't know what's the matter with you. I carry you all over the place, and you have the back seat. I get lots more loving than you and I got the front seat. You got to kid and joke with 'em, get right in there to get your sugar. You either got to change your stuff or you ain't ever going to do any good with the sweetie pies."

I started to tell him that what he should now kiss was my ass, but checked myself in tribute to future double dates. Cars weren't that easy to come by, and Ernie could be touchy. But I did have to change my style. I knew it—and that's what made me so mad, his knowing it. I bought a flaming maroon-and-gold school jacket, feeling embarrassed the first time I strolled down the hall in it. And then accustomed to it, only took it off to sleep. I must be noticed! I joined the Debating Society, without a try out, under the fluttering, absent-minded hand of Miss Godsey. On our first field trip, pitted against the greased tongues of Training School (RESOLVED: One World or No World), I strode like a shot to the podium, gazed down on a sea of happy, expectant faces, and then—terror-stricken at my audacity—started a strangled discourse that made absolutely no sense. My next time out was slightly better, but our Debating Society did not win one match that year. I got off wisecracks in class every time I could get away with it. I sent Meredith Christmas, Valentine, and Easter cards—with short snappy notes attached. And, during the summer before our senior year, on a vacation to Washington, D.C., I inscribed in Glen Echo Park a disc that was designed for identification: BONES LOVES L'L MEREDITH.

And then there was that activity that dwarfed all others, that received the eyes of all the town. If I could only be a hero there. Sports.

Three

I do not remember learning how to speak, and I do not know when I first learned to play football. For as far back as I can remember there was always some kind of ball available for a game. Before organized sports began and adults gained full control, we made our own rules and enforced them. There was "touch" football (which we told our mothers we would play) and there was "tackle" (which we actually played).

After school from the earliest days on—and all day Saturday and half on Sunday—we chose sides on the vacant lot and lit into each other like savages. The boundaries for play were things like a footpath to the right, an old oak tree to the left—touchdowns, going over a hill toward my house and making it to the sidewalk at the opposite end. When the Sheik hit my house occasionally on a goal-line plunge—four or five lightweights clinging to every moving part—the structure would shake to its foundation and the windows rattle; my aunt would then appear and say, "Now, Dude!" It was a reference to *Tobacco Road* where Dude had a habit of tossing a ball against his house. (My family had a stock of literary references most people could not understand; the Sheik thought on this occasion that someone named Dude was getting blamed and was relieved.) Arguments broke out constantly over whether someone had stepped out of bounds or if a tackle had been completed before some flying ninety-pound frame had hurtled over the hill for a score. ("A tackle, a TACKLE!" "NO, my pant leg touched the ground but my knee never. SCORE!")

A referee was what we needed, but only the sickly—those with no desire to bang heads and gain fame—would accept the responsibility, and mainly they had trouble enforcing their decisions. We felt them inept. Not so, though, with Arnold Jaggers. A permanently pale boy who built crystal radios and complicated erector sets, he served as referee from time to time, using a whistle and sticking his fragile, tubercular head right into the line of scrimmage. Our mythology seemed to need at least one learned figure like him around, a saintlike soul who was above our everyday world and who could hand down Socratic judgments. "That Arnold knows everything in the world about football. There's nothing he don't know. If he could play the game, he'd kill us all."

His world of knowledge and crystal sets, of being pale and awkward, was a foreign land—and, consequently, something to distrust and scorn at first. But what a giddy and warm feeling came to you when you could find reasons to make him a buddy. (We learned to hate the Germans and Japanese, too, and that same giddy feeling struck when we found a good word to say about them. Ditto, the colored; when the Langston High Glee Club appeared annually on stage at assembly —three rows of dark faces in black robes and white wing collars—everyone from our principal on down melted in good will. "Boy, they sure raise the roof on that 'Go Down, Moses.' Can't nobody sing like them!")

And Arnold continued his surprises to the end. There we had been putting him down as a sissy, someone to poke when you had nothing else to do, and on the Turner brothers' back porch one summer night—nothing much else to do—he had unwound a wang for inspection that went down like a firehose. One of the Turner brothers—fixated on all mechanisms of sex, nothing too outlandish or obscure for him—had said, as if asking a gifted pianist friend to play a number for the homefolk, "Go on, show the guys your rod, Arnold. They ain't going to believe it." After a little coaxing, he did so. And down the line we passed, looking at it and shaking our heads in disbelief. The Sheik had a great respect for Arnold after that, predicting a brilliant future for him and following his career closely. Arnold became a minister of the gospel.

On the field of play we learned that courage counted most. Those who had the guts to tackle "low"—around flying ankles and chugging knees—were respected, while the ones who liked painlessly to bring down the ball-carrier by climbing aboard his shoulders or slinging him at the waist were considered flawed and weak no matter what their bulk or swagger. I tackled low; what did a broken nose or a ringing in the head matter if you had your buddies' awe and respect. The only thing that gave me pause ever was teeth, my mother being crazed about their good care. "Look," she would say when we were at a movie together, "the good men all have shiny white teeth. The bad men have bad teeth." I learned early, too, that the spectacular and unexpected gained unbounded attention and could minimize deficiencies. On kickoffs to the opposite side I sailed down field ahead of the pack —an eighty-eight-pound blur of light—and leaped at the flying feet of the receiver. "That Boney's as crazy as a coot," they said. That was a high compliment; and with their respect, I could then direct my team.

When we had the ball, I liked to pick out someone on the opposing side—preferably someone tough and big on the outside, vulnerable on the inside—and run the play directly at him, yours truly toting the leather. I took the snap, tucked the scarred ball against my belly, and ran at the victim at full tilt with my eyes closed. If I allowed myself to look into his startled and bewildered eyes, I knew I would feel sorry for him and not do the job. I could often feel him going over on his back, with a low moan—or, sometimes, in a side step he would place an arm around my neck, at which point a quick elbow into his gut would spring me free.

Grownups—those slow moving and indulgently smiling creatures—often watched from the sidelines, many times giving unwanted advice. On rare occasions one would step in to direct an attack, throwing the ball too hard for our fingers to catch or thinking up complicated, Statue-of-Liberty-type plays that no one could follow. They seemed to need living proof that they could move back into our world any time they wanted, as if it were a retreat they always had a right to; on the other hand, they guarded all their preserves and rituals as if no one would ever be old and wise enough to penetrate them. Yet how old, I came to ask myself much later, does one have to be to finally get rid of the playground? When a Kennedy called on us for more "vigor," when a Johnson laid it on the line and told the boys to "bring back that coonskin and tack it on the wall," I felt the stirring of fall afternoons with

66

the smell of rubbed leather and the sense of a ringing head. Seeing a president pop up spectacularly and unexpectedly to announce a trip to China or a total economic freeze, and I am again racing down the vacant lot on kickoff to surprise friend and foe alike. And just let me glimpse a Reverend Billy Graham hovering somewhere in the background, toothy smile and in a better suit than I've ever worn, and I instinctively tap my wallet and look around to make sure the womenfolk are safe. Boys, I have been there before.

And live long enough and the unexpected is acted upon you, instead of the other way around.

One Saturday afternoon a new set of faces suddenly loomed by the old oak tree. All colored, our age. They didn't ask to play, showed no sign of emotion at our own play, just stood there mute and apparent, heads high. The rules we lived by didn't allow games between white and colored. Occasionally, older boys or men who weren't working would barrel at night into Potliquor, the cluster of weather-beaten frame houses, to—as the phrase went—"put the niggers in their place." (No one thought to question the fact that, in Potliquor, they were in their "place" already.) The prefight fervor was akin to the emotion that went through the stands before a high school football game with arch-rival Kingstown, a place only eighteen miles away but which could have been the Isle of Nippon for any love or compassion showered upon it by us. The Kingstown players were subhuman to us, maniacs in oddly colored uniforms with strange marching songs and sly, cunning maneuvers.

Goddamn Kingstown, we're goin' to whup their asses! And the big colored boys and their men out of work, lounging in front of the Potliquor grocery store and barbershop, presented the same kind of bizarreness, something just meant to fight and conquer. The fact that the colored were just as big and strong as our side, possibly a little more so, added to the challenge. If you could whup a nigger or stand him down with all the devices he had at hand—the dreaded straight razor leading the list—then you could walk proudly among your peers although unemployed and crippled and defeated in so many other ways.

Ted Lundsford, who had only recently been a star football player before losing a leg due to injuring and reinjuring it in the game, led unique raids into Potliquor. He would pass through the poolroom in that creaky, dipping walk he had, not quite master yet of his new artificial leg, calling on everyone who wasn't a coward to follow. In Potliquor, a gaggle of whites behind him and looking at the ground, he would creak up toward the grocery store/barbershop. He still looked much the same as he did before the "operation": hair black and curly, his athlete's neck thick, biceps bulging in his T-shirt. An unsmiling colored person, a leader you could tell, would amble up to Ted before he got to the door. Standing still, Ted's artificial leg splayed out to the side like an elephantine cane.

"Get out of my way," Ted would say.

"Now don't you come messing around if you're looking for trouble. Just a warning. I'll whup you good."

There was the interminable period of their silently staring at each other. One would spit to the side, then the other. They talked about how they would fight, like Ernie Peoples describing diddling his thirteen-year-old in a furnace room, so graphically and with such an eye for detail, that a real fight couldn't possibly touch it. "I'll beat your head up against that post till it splinters," Ted would say. The colored man laughed; the only one to do so. "Why, I'll throw you up on this here roof and you'll never get down with that dead leg," he shot back.

They then went over ground rules calmly, almost politely. "No knives or sticks," Ted said.

"Don't worry," the colored man said.

"And you can't call your buddies in."

"Won't have to. We'll fight for half an hour. Somebody here can time us."

"Let's just say when somebody gives up. When he's had enough and knows he's whupped. . . ."

I never saw Ted fight although I did see him feint with his left once and cock back his right; the colored man ducked and started forward—until they started talking again. One night I actually saw Ted make it into the grocery store, swinging his artificial leg around in an arc going up the plank steps. He dipped and creaked past men with stocking caps on their heads, slits cut in the side of their shoes to favor bunions, and razor-fight scars on their necks and cheeks. He'd done it, he'd gone into No Man's Land! We could see him inside, big as life, swigging a Nehi and eating a Moon Pie. In the car rattling back to the poolroom, he said, "Did I stand them niggers down or didn't I . . . ?"

Now a knot of colored boys stood waiting, watching our sandlot game. When we were ready to play them, we didn't have to put it in words. We simply pointed to the opposite end of the vacant lot—toward my house—and the colored boys trotted down there. They acted shy, not looking us full in the face, rubbing their hands down the sides of their pants, giving brief, rapid-fire directions to each other. New meat! And there was no doubt that our side could take them. The Sheik outweighed any two of them put together, and I just knew that a shoestring tackle or two would take the fight out of them. What if games between us were frowned upon by the outside; we could get in plenty of plays before our mothers caught us—if we hurried. The Sheik held, and I booted deep. A tall, gangling boy—someone I heard called Duke—took the kick and paused a moment. If he didn't know how to play, I was sure going to teach him. He took a few hesitant steps, holding the ball in his hands; I dived into his feet, bringing him down in a mushroom of dust. The colored boys huddled, still wiping their hands on their pants, not smiling or saying a word to us yet. They ran four times and lost yardage, the Sheik and I using a flashy two-on-one—one high and one low—to cut the runner down. We chattered a lot after each tackle, slapping each other on the butt. It felt eerie, an adventure, to touch their wiry hair, and we thought we could smell a musky, but not unpleasant, odor from them. Silence still from our new opponents. Then we got the ball. "O.K., I'll take it around left end," I said in the huddle, feeling the excitement of taking charge and going first.

The old familiar ball tucked chest high, eyes shut when I cut as always, I felt myself suddenly going head over heels in a complete circle. Even before I hit the ground full-force on my back, before my breath left and stars floated from eyes, ears, nose and mouth, I knew I had made some kind of horrible mistake. And I had made it even before I had taken the ball to carry. Although I had trouble seeing and moving my right shoulder, I jumped up. If still conscious, you always had to jump up. Then I heard it—really what I had been waiting for without knowing it. The colored boys were laughing—big cackles. "Duke, you really bring him down. Now we really going murder them."

"O.K., Sheik," in the huddle. "You take it right up the middle."

"You're crazy, Boney. I ain't running against them guys."

"O.K., I'll go to the right this time." Never again, I told

myself, would I be a leader; this was what came of it. "Now block that guy Duke."

Around to the right I set sail—as far to the right as I could make it—ball clutched low in my nearly paralyzed arm. Out of the corner of my eye I could see the Sheik brush against Duke, and then they were on me, Duke in the center and around my middle. They were not skillful or trained in tackling, but they had a nervous, desperate vitality that was gaining terrible momentum. They got up, whooping and beating dust from their trousers in my face. Now I felt warm blood oozing from a knee under my pants. What hurt most, though, was the memory of how cocky and confident I had been at the start, the pathetic chatter and show-off maneuvers. "Boys, we got to try a pass," I said in the huddle.

"O.K., you throw it. You're the quarterback."

I had to sling it, feeling the snorts from four impassive black faces as they came charging in, from a sidearm position, unable to lift my right shoulder. The ball flew over everyone's head somehow, high, right against the tin roof of my house. A moment later, my mother stood in the side door. "Johnny, don't you think you should come in now? Dinner's almost ready."

"Aw, Momma . . ."

You could never quit when hurt, never ever when you were being beat—but a call from Home overruled all. The rules said so. I trotted away from the field, trying not to limp, holding my paralyzed shoulder as high as I could, tasting blood and grit and defeat. "Sorry, guys, I got to quit. Go on without me." Saved once again by Home!

But the colored boys came back to play on other days. They stood by the oak tree, not quite so content anymore to wait silently and respectfully for an invitation. If a ball fell anywhere near them, they grabbed it and were soon in the game. They argued now over whether someone had stepped out of bounds, if the goal line had been crossed or if one team was offside. Argued and spit and kicked sod on us. They didn't play, as we called it, "dirty," slugging someone covertly to a fare-thee-well after he was already down—but then they didn't have to. They kept knocking us here and there like ten-pins, and our strategy—mine—was to keep from being thrown on our necks as much as possible and try for delays and time-consuming plays that kept their score to a minimum. And just wait for our mommas to mercifully ring the dinner bell or call us in for chores.

Duke—tall, somber-miened, skin the color of slate—continued to lead his side and picked me out from the first as his victim. I was the leader, i.e., the loudmouth, of the opposition. His Sancho was a short, squat, moon-faced boy they called Jiggs—skin as dark as night—and he egged Duke on to a higher rage (and me to fight back more against my better judgment). "Duke he going throw that white Boney cross the street if he take the ball. That Boney can't gain one inch on old Duke." Of course I had to carry the ball after that, and an inch was about all I did gain.

And then football was not enough. One day I brought out the boxing gloves for some vacant lot sparring, and the colored phalanx hovered by the oak tree a brief moment before poking their heads over our shoulders. "Duke he can whup that white Boney," Jiggs said. "That white Boney's scared to put on the gloves with Duke."

"Come on, Duke," I said then. "Put 'em on."

It pleased me to note a little concern on his face, some caution. It was perhaps the first time he had ever put on boxing gloves. He watched raptly as Jiggs, ever helpful, scooted them up his hands and then laced them. Duke beat them together and moved tentatively toward me. The others, white and colored, formed a circle around us—hiding us from grown-up eyes. Now I was by God going to get him, lay into him for all the taunts and times I'd been made to eat dust. In boxing—as in the other sports—initial surprise was the weapon I had learned to count on most; daring to do what no one else would do, and quickly. I flew into him, landing a haymaker to the side of his head. It was a right, cocked back as far as I could reach and sent home with all my eighty-eight-pound strength. That should do it. But, no, he came back. Awkwardly, mouth and eyes fully open, swinging like a windmill. The eyes were always what killed me in fights; to look into an opponent's eyes and see hurt or anger or fear drained the sap right out of me. It made the person all too human, made me see myself in him, and made everything finally too naked and revealing. My perfect match would probably have been a blind man.

"Don't let him get away with it, Duke," Jiggs was yelling. "Beat him into the ground. Make him eat them gloves!"

Duke found that the best way to fight me was in a half-slugging, half-wrestling way. It was hard to explain to him—while being choked in a half-nelson—that boxing didn't permit such clinches. And none of my buddies came to my aid when he began his wrestling—not the Sheik, Pancho, anyone. It made me feel, sadly, that they didn't mind seeing me get beat, too. Thrown to the ground once, a couple of wild punches finding their way to my head—and relief came at last from the old stand-by: *"Johnny, dinner!"* But in trotting off, carrying the gloves by their string, I threw back a taunt at Duke: "Get you next time. And I'll make sure we fight fair then." The cackles at my back didn't keep me from imagining a proper bout out behind the barn, Firehose Arnold with his whistle, keeping Duke from wrestling and making sure the rounds were three minutes.

A few weeks later it seemed strange that I could have thought about such a standard, refereed fight. Duke began working as a shoeshine boy downtown, and he moved the arena for our battles onto Main Street. He would spot me— dressed in a white shirt, face washed, a dime or so in my pockets for a movie and candy—and run out to pin me against a wall. He babbled in a wild, highly agitated manner —scary just to behold—making demands and solidifying my victim state. "You, Boney, I need fifteen cents, you got fifteen cents, gimme fifteen cents, gimme it now, come on, gimme, gimme . . ."

I was startled at first, and strangely felt guilty, although he was doing the beating up. My shirt was too clean next to his, all the love and concern I had at home was obviously much more than he had, and I could go in the Majestic where the rules forbade him to. I was thankful he couldn't follow me there—for now he had the Indian Sign on me. He would cork me on the shoulder to warm up, butt me with his head, and my only defense was retreat. No, I wanted to explain, downtown is where we go to movies, to buy things in department stores—it's not to play vacant lot games on. And, as my head bopped back against brick and coins were clawed out of my pocket, I thought the grownups might have known what they were doing after all—as they did about other things once in a great while. That one invitation to play football, and now my back was being pummeled as I streaked toward the haven of the Majestic.

Duke and his sidekick Jiggs were not like any colored people I'd ever met before. They weren't like Flossie and her girls who cleaned and helped out at our house on Saturdays, eating at the table with us, fussing and arguing and always so kind. They weren't like Jujube, the janitor at school, ruling his territory and so funny with jokes; nor like Eustace, who hung around the drugstore and got you to run errands and buy ice cream for him because you liked him so much. Some bit of chemistry was working away in Duke and Jiggs that wasn't such a strong potion in the others, white or black. I got just the barest taste of that potion once when I found Albert Van Landingham—big-assed and a piano player—to poke on after school in the eighth grade. The need to strike out came on the wave of puberty, so many forces threatening me, so much unknown and bewildering and unfair. And there was Albert Van Landingham to weathervane my anger, to allow the heady elixir of making someone else take punishment to rise. I would beat him on the chubby arm, say, "Take that, you fat-assed ivory tinkler," and relish the cringe before me. A few years later, adolescent woes battened down for the time being and the music of Tschaikovsky discovered, I tried to be friends with Albert, to make him see I was made of finer stuff than a bully. He went through the motions—but those eyes, the windows of the soul. They said he would never forget.

Beyond the sandlot games lay the organized sports—like marriage waiting after days of freewheeling carousal. There they had coaches, referees in striped shirts, a scoreboard, and heroes. When the curtain first opened on this stage, there I stood in line—air heavy with sweat, the scent of uniforms kept interminably in storage, damp concrete, and fear—to receive padded khaki knickers, bulky shoulder pads, and a white jersey. A member of the Junior High Midgets only had to supply football shoes, something I wheedled my mother into buying as a matter of life and death. And then we of the Midgets—the lowest of the low, the smallest of the small—trotted to a faraway stretch of practice field that wouldn't be claimed by the High School Varsity—the highest of the high —or by other teams who took preference over boys who had to weigh under a hundred pounds or else weren't supposed to play on the squad.

On our own territory we performed every ritual the older, bigger boys did—only in miniature. "O.K., team," Coach Travis said, "let's all do the Jumping Jack." He himself, of course, did not jump out, clapping his hands above him, shooting out his legs. He was a dignified man with wavy hair, a slightly pigeon-toed walk, an adult who wore a tie and business suit on the field. His eyes were going over all of us, a clipboard in his hand, and each of us was trying desperately to find a skill and way for him to take special note. To make the team, to bring that honor home—worthy enough to call oneself a Midget—was something that would surely pale every other accomplishment in life. "O.K., gang, give 'em all you got," I screamed, impressed by chants I'd heard the Varsity use. "Let's fight, fight, fight!"

"Shut up, Boney," a moody friend said, beside me. "This is the warm-up. We ain't started playing yet."

We were taught to get down in blocking stance, tested to see who could get between two blockers and bring down a runner head-on; and given wind sprint after wind sprint that tore the breath and near life out of you. "Dig, dig," and we fought to carry out some assignment, to do it better than the next boy in competition. In sandlot we played all positions. Here the coach told you where to play—at pulling guard, halfback, or pass-snagging end—and it was up to you to catch his eye. Sometimes the ball would be going one way and your assignment would take you far away—to belt a defensive back at the opposite end. But you must never let up, had to use all the flair you had, for no telling where Coach Travis' walleye might be. And soon he would announce the Starting Eleven. God.

On my bike, after practice one day, I encountered the Sheik by the vacant lot. His weight had kept him from trying for the Midgets, and he was too young for the Varsity. "I'm never going to make it," I said. "I'll never make the team. Never, never. I ain't good enough."

"What you want, Boney, is for me to tell you that you're *going* to make it," he said, in a strangely level tone. "That's why you keep going on about not having a chance. Well, I'm onto you."

"No, I'll swear . . ." What shamed me was that he had seen right through me, had known all along how crazed I was to be a Midget. If he'd told me, Yes, he agreed, I'd never make the team in a million years, it wouldn't have bothered me nearly as much as his zeroing in on my private thoughts. It didn't occur to me that he might be grumpy because he was too fat to even try out.

A week before the Kingstown game, at the start of practice, Coach Travis tucked his clipboard against his hip and pointed to first one boy and another. "You there Jenkins. I want you over there at left end." It came so dramatically, with such force, that we didn't have to ask what this meant. Some boys had been assured of positions, their faces radiating such confidence that no doubt could ever exist that they wouldn't be picked. They would go through life that way, being doctors, lawyers, coaches and fathers themselves, fitting into place as easily as a knife into butter, even dying in regular, unmessy ways. But now, for some, the inevitable surprises. ". . . And now for pulling guard, I want that fellow right there to go in. You." He was pointing at me. A mistake? They'd never know it. I frowned, nodded, and then took off for the position between the tackle and center as if nothing could have been more normal. "The rest of you boys—some a lot bigger— may wonder why I've picked this little fellow for the starting team," the coach went on. "I'll tell you. He never quits. I've watched him after a play has been blown dead and he's still in there fighting. You could all learn from him, all you bigger boys."

The days before the Kingstown game passed in a delirium. Running plays with the Starting Eleven in scrimmage, I pulled back after the snap from center and took off around one end or the other like a bat out of hell, diving into the first mass of convenient bodies I could find. No one was quite sure—even Coach Travis—as to why a guard had to pull around end all the time. And losing oneself immediately in a downed jumble of bodies seemed a little pointless. But the great Vols of the University of Tennessee, under Coach Bob Neyland, had a pulling guard, and now the Midgets must have one, too. At night I would at first try iodine and then put Mercurochrome on bleeding knees that were constantly losing scabs. So much medicine had gone on, so many scabs lost, that finally a scent, which I took for the start of gangrene, began to emanate from there. Oh, God, I prayed in bedtime prayers, please let me play through the season before I lose my legs.

Even the weather seemed different the day of the Kingstown Game, as it was the first day of a school year. The sun shone in a cloudless blue sky, breaking through the cafeteria windows to warm us as we tried to force down an early hamburger. It was impossible to concentrate in any class—and at every bell I swung into the lavatory to pee in excitement. I saw footballs soaring, time-outs with the team and coach conferring, the strange city and field we would soon invade. After years it seemed, our Tennessee history teacher said, at one thirty in the afternoon: "The boys on the Midget Team are excused now. They are to report to the gymnasium."

Those eyes on the few of us as we ambled out! We were going off to awesome adventures; they were stuck there, learning once again about how John Sevier in a far-off time had fought the Indians. *So long, I'm moving ahead of you!* In the gym we were to take a "physical" before boarding two dump trucks that would take us to Kingstown. A doctor in a suit, a stethoscope around his neck, was seated on the edge of a straight-back chair at one end. A swivel-necked lamp, brightly lit, stood on a table beside him. Our team moved slowly, one by one, in front of him. Just like the big boys did, and guys going into the army. It was scary as hell. "What's he going to do to us?" I asked the boy in front.

"He feels your balls and you cough. That's it."

I tried out several coughs along the way. In front of him I smiled. If he likes me, he'll pass me. My pants lowered, boxer shorts to my knees, he placed a finger beside my scrotum and pushed upward. I coughed, he nodded. Then the other side. He wrote something down as I buttoned myself back in place. He said nothing. I raised my BVD undershirt, and he placed the cold silver nozzle of his stethoscope hard on my chest. I looked at the glint it picked up from the swivel-necked lamp. He went high on my chest and low, straight across and back. Then he motioned for me to turn around and he went to work with it on my back. I looked at the line of boys from that position and tried to smile. He placed his hand on my shoulder and I turned back around. His hand, I noted, was warm. He spoke. "Son, don't put your uniform on today. You've got a little something there."

"What, sir?"

"A little murmur. Nothing serious. You just shouldn't play today."

Like all doctors, he seemed pressed for time and motioned for the next boy to step forward. I felt ashamed; something inside me, something I'd lived with all these years without seeing, had proved unworthy. I found Coach Travis on the running track above, clipboard at the ready, directing boys finished with the exam to the roaring dump trucks outside. He took the news almost humorously. Was he glad to have this chance to move another into my position? And he certainly didn't have to wait long for volunteers. While I stood before him, my expensive football shoes tied by laces over my arm, a tall, swarthy boy (later destined for leadership in the local crime syndicate) moved in for the kill. "Coach, I know all his plays. You want me to start?"

"I don't—"

"You got to start somebody, and I can do it! Start me!"

"Well, O.K." Just like that.

And hard on his heels was someone after me: A poor boy —quiet, good-natured—who had had to practice in brogans because his family couldn't afford football shoes. He played the other guard position. "Boney, you ain't going to be using them shoes anymore. Would you let me use 'em today?"

"Sure, why not."

They were a trifle large for him, the toes sticking up and swaying in the middle. But he was proud of them—prouder even than I had been—reaching down to touch them as the dump truck we squatted in roared and bounced the eighteen miles to Kingstown. I was being permitted to accompany the team in my street clothes, not knowing where to go or how to act. We were taught how to win and lose at football, what to think about school grades—but no one had ever said a word about heart trouble. What did a heart murmur do? Was I going to have a heart attack and die?

The dump trucks careened into a high weed area beside which lay a green-grass football field with white goal posts and down from it a low shadowy school building. Students— our own age, strangers—were moving about, schoolbooks cradled against chest by the girls, held to the hip by the boys. Just as we did it. I saw in my mind thousands of swirls, like stars in the night, spread out all across the country, each of us playing the same games but with different characters and shape of terrain. Kingstown was Mars, and I jumped to its earth for the first time from the dump truck. I wondered what life would have been like growing up here. Lots better, I thought. It was like imagining life after death.

We beat Kingstown that day. After being nothing to noth-ing right up to the last seconds of the last quarter, Tuffie Brown, who lived around the corner from me and was re-puted to have screwed his next-door neighbor in a henhouse, caught a grandstander over his left shoulder and flat-footed it into the end zone. They whooped about that last play all the way home, the fact that they had made it up in the huddle, that a defensive back had tripped at the last second, and that Tuffie had never been able to hold onto a pass in his life be-fore. That play fulfilled everything: The boys had thought it up, not the coach; luck had been on our side; and a proven loser—Butterfingers Tuffie—had snagged one when it counted most. I was still thinking about the first play, though. The opening kickoff—my specialty. I had seen the ball sail end over end and plop snugly into a Kingstown player's arm. Our team had come racing down, right into flying legs, el-bows, and concussion-causing knees. The ball-carrier had then disappeared under seven or eight bodies, part theirs, part ours.

Their players looked stronger and had more decisive moves. If I had been in on that kickoff, I knew I would have been the first down there on that strange carrier, the littlest of the little, the first leaper into the meat grinder. It was my way, my grandstander, to be first. Thank you, dear God, I had prayed from the sidelines, for the heart murmur and keeping me from death on the kickoff. Our Southern Baptist religion had taught us that the Lord worked in mysterious ways, His wonders to perform. He must have spent some time thinking this one up.

And our family doctor—old Doc Gallimore, with drooping, melancholy eyes like a hound dog's—could find no trace of a murmur when my mother took me to him. In the grand tradition of American medicine, he had an entirely different diagnosis. "His heart is as sound as a gold watch," he said. "If he were my boy, I'd let him play."

But by this time the tall, swarthy boy who had a brilliant future in crime awaiting him had nailed down my old position. No matter what, though, you had to continue. Examples were everywhere that only death stopped the game. Bells Jamieson, an older boy, had his brains knocked loose by the mighty Trojans of Knoxville; a block had turned him groggy, he was resting on one knee, when the ball-carrier ran over his head. Out on a stretcher, but no matter. Next season he was back with a specially padded helmet—much larger than regular ones—running and directing plays when he could remember them. Jitterbug Watson had epileptic seizures on the field and still stayed in there. A play would sometimes end and Jitterbug wouldn't get up. No one had hit him, he had simply dropped. Sometimes he would drop in the huddle. An emergency team would then trot out and pull his tongue and he would be back in there fighting in no time.

And with a blank check from one doctor on my heart, I

was diving back in myself. I played Pee Wee basketball that winter. We arose well before sunup and practiced while stars still shone in the sky, for this was the only period—except maybe midnight—when no one else bigger could lay claim to the court. The Pee Wees were the last in line. And I played on the second team, stumbling in with other unfortunates only when the outcome of a game was already determined. But it was my last season to be a Midget, Pee Wee, or to ever go by a diminutive term—except in derision—for almost overnight after the last Pee Wee goal was sunk I began to grow like a weed gone wild. Everything was sprouting to great lengths except, unfortunately, my tool—leaving me exhausted as if in fever. But I dived back in, of course, grasping for any life preserver that floated past. By the time Meredith Lancaster had come along, I was into the most minute branch of sports in high school, the tennis team. We played without cheerleaders, with a coach who took us to matches in a 1927 Dodge that had window shades and was chronically breaking down, and we rolled down our own courts and furnished all equipment. All white on court? We wore bathing trunks and khaki short pants, no shirts ever and high-top black Keds. But wouldn't Meredith ever walk by, in that cute way she had, books up against her chest, eyes wide, five miles out of town —and see me just once make an overhead smash? All six-foot-two, 117 pounds of me? No, not once.

The Friday night football game was where you would find her, everyone, all of us assigned different roles.

Lights blazed down on the green, white-striped field, so strong that dew could be seen glistening and growing on the grass. The thick, gray goal posts were made of iron, a substance the authorities believed couldn't be torn apart in post-game frenzy. It got expensive replacing wooden ones after every game. In the stands we sat, parents nervously fidgeting with their hands, lonely ex-athletes with pot guts, girls primly upright, eyes expectant, businessmen who advertised their wares in the game program, boys too melancholy to be cheerleaders, too off-key or embarrassed to toot a horn, too frail or inept or smart to be down there in the arena with their muscle and bone and cunning put to the ultimate test.

The cheerleaders raced out first, dressed in the school colors of maroon and gold. Meredith Lancaster led the pack, her long legs pale in the bright light, twirling so that her gold cheerleader panties were right there for all the world to see. Ernie Peoples brought up the rear, his wavy red hair flashing with Vitalis that could be sniffed in the first three rows, throwing himself into an inexpert cartwheel. The referees strolled out, building tension. Then the band broke out into "Fight, Wildcats, Fight!" and the team, in clean, unmarked uniforms, trotted past the cinder track and onto the field. The game began, with the drummer doing a guillotine-roll as the kickoff sailed.

The Sheik—weight now an asset—played in the line. He couldn't move, I saw—but, more importantly, no one else could move him either. A pride of blockers bounced off him, the runner ricocheting down to the side. His contribution was all-important but unspectacular, and you had to be a friend in the stands to even notice him. He never got to touch the ball except in a fumble. But Pancho. My good old buddy Pancho. As he had done in pool-hustling and high-board diving, he suddenly came up with a desperate skill no one would have suspected. He caught passes—impossible, unbelievable passes.

In the end zone he would leap over the backs of enemy players and snag them with one hand over his shoulder. He dived full-face and somehow always came up with the ball tucked neatly at his middle. No one could cover him, and I could understand the enemy's frustration. When Pancho wanted something—the football, to sink the nine ball, to be the high-board diving champ—he was inhumanly hungry for it, as if his very life depended upon it. He knew this vulnerability, though, and only got interested when things got down to brass tacks and when he knew he stood a chance. He was a poor student because he knew his strengths did not lie there. Why knock yourself out to be just mediocre? He had been a lackadaisical sandlot player. What had it mattered there? But now here was something important—with the whole town watching, the band playing, girls cheering. And he *wanted* more than any of us. And he never got hurt on the field.

Ernie Peoples was the first casualty of the football season our senior year. After Pancho had snagged a forty-yarder, turned a flip, and held onto the ball, Ernie flew into an extemporaneous half-flip, half-cartwheel, throwing his knee painfully out of place. Poor old Ernie. They had to carry him out on a stretcher. And our team in maroon and gold lost. Coach C. W. Ballew, a tough, unsmiling man, who knocked out players with his bare fists when displeased and emulated the University of Tennessee in everything—the Single Wing, pushing players past all endurance, playing for keeps—copying them in everything except one thing: He couldn't win. Pancho was not enough to carry the day. But the contest didn't end with the final whistle. There was always the post-game fistfight between partisans. Misshapen youths and men bordering on forty who still wore school colors lay into one another like Visigoths under a streetlight near the stadium. Anyone you hadn't seen before, who must therefore be from the other side, was fair game. They had their best streetfighters, and we had ours—and the side that still had someone standing under the streetlight when the police arrived was the winner. We usually won there. And as a parting gesture to the visiting side we had a special team that would urinate in the gas tanks of all cars with out-of-town tags.

On Saturday and Sunday the sports pages were filled with the exploits of Friday night, often now featuring photos of Pancho leaping for a catch. And on Monday those who had played the game moved down halls and into classes, proudly sporting adhesive over eyebrows, arms in slings, limps. The nonplaying boys treated them respectfully with a little tinge of fear, and the girls fluttered their eyelashes downward.

But Pancho—the hero of them all—still didn't know how to treat girls. I saw him—see him now—grabbing one of Meredith's textbooks just before she walked into class. The bell was primed to ring, she had to have the book—what did he think he was doing? Her eyes widened, mad. "Pancho, give me my book. Give it here. Now!"

She took off hotly around a corner after him while he hooted. Girls won't like you when you do something like that. It didn't go with Harry Horlick's music or Van Johnson movies or the sonnets of William Shakespeare. Meredith, so classy, so above everything, making me blush every time I got near her, must detest that kind of treatment.

Now wouldn't you have thought so?

Four

But then came the day I waited to walk home with Pancho after school. We never had to make formal arrangements for getting together—a procedure called for on a nerve-racking date—it was just taken for granted. That was what was so great about being buddies, nothing tense, everything familiar. It was a Monday, the football team had lost by only one point on Friday, making it seem almost a victory, and no practice was called this day. I sat on the concrete slab down from the entrance, books I'd never study jiggling on my knee, my ass freezing, waiting for the saloon doors to part and Pancho to come hunching forward, hands deep in pockets, brooding in that way he had. Maybe we'd run off a rack at the Buffalo, bump into the Sheik and get a few laughs.

Did he have to "stay in" for an added half-hour, punishment for talking in study hall or something? Everybody else was flying through the doors. Ernie Peoples limped up on his cheerleader-torn knee, wanting to go for a shake. We both knew, even before he asked, that I wouldn't accept. Too tame. A stout girl who sat next to me in physics lingered my way for a second. She was always lingering, slipping me notes, blushing. That would never do. I'd done nothing to deserve it—except exist. It was somehow flattering, though, and I felt a sort of affection for her. Now where the hell was Pancho?

Over my shoulder I caught a glimpse of raven-black hair, neatly parted and wet from a recent combing. He was strolling, not hunching forward this time, down the narrow drive beside the school that was obscured by a wall and greenery. Why there? It was secluded, private. He should be doing like everybody else, taking the steps. But of course I knew. Already I felt the emotion start to flash, like a fire's first crackle. It was so fresh, so awesome—my first experience of it—I couldn't help for a moment just being impressed by its force. That was Meredith Lancaster he was walking beside. *My* Meredith. And throughout the run of emotion, my ass was freezing itself off on the slab. I couldn't help being impressed by that fact of nature, too. No matter what, the body kept going its way.

I took off down the steps, telling myself not to follow them when I got to the foot. Don't be a fool. They cut toward Main Street, Pancho poking her and saying something that made her bark out in a mock indignant voice. She wore her R.O.T.C. Sponsor's blue uniform, white socks, and those adored, scuffed saddle-oxfords. They seemed headed for the Chocolate Bar. I swung around the railroad tracks and ended up, naturally, in the Buffalo, where I immediately took on the Sheik in a game of straight ball. The new emotion, almost delicious in its strength the way a fever was, burning up past conceits, so completely took charge that I didn't think about the game and won hands down. Thinking was what killed me in pool. "Boney, you're the luckiest son of a bitch that ever lived," the Sheik said. "Finally, you always win."

Little things now kept dropping from Pancho which caused my heart to sink. But I just couldn't be mad at him. Years before old Dumbrute Shelton, a fine buddy who lived in the country, had got "the hairs" before I did. I had got so mad I stopped speaking to him for a year. You learn, though. When something is destined, you have to accept it in the end, so why not clear the decks and do it in the beginning? *Le roi est mort, vive le roi!* Pancho tuned in music on the radio now when he took me for a ride in Uncle Buford's V-8. "Quiet, shut up," he would hiss. "It's 'Sentimental Journey.' . . ." And when its last bar died, he sang, head raised, eyes moist, so off-key you wouldn't know the song unless it'd just played,

> *Goin' take that sent-ti-ment-tul jour-ney*
> *Goin' ta set my heart at ease. . . .*

"How come you like that song?"

"I don't know. I never knew those kind of songs were so nice before."

Before what? And one Sunday morning I turned over in bed, seeing Pancho striding out on the street in a suit, tie, and polished shoes. The son of a bitch was heading for the Presbyterian church. *Meredith's* church. And to cap everything off, he started giving me advice on how to live. Me, who could read a book through and had been to Washington, D.C. "The Sheik and them kind of guys are all right at first, but after awhile you'll see their lives ain't heading any place." He was sounding like a Scout Master, a sellout, my buddy Pancho. "They'll get you in real big trouble, too, if you don't watch out."

That chance for trouble came shortly. The Sheik came running, like a mirage growing real, down the vacant lot for my house. Knees pumping out to the side, arms pile driving. The only time I'd ever seen him run like that was when he'd stolen something and someone was after him. Was he on the lam? Was I supposed to hide him out now in the house until the heat blew over—in our place where meals came on time, jokes were so complex in origin they always needed translation to outsiders, and where you could spend hours in the toilet in peace and read a novel through? But the Sheik didn't want to come in. He asked my mother at the side door—in that beguiling, respectful tone we used around adults—if I was there and could come out. No, he'd just stand there on the steps and wait. But please tell me to hurry. In the backyard, under the apple tree that produced the hardest, most inedible fruit in Tennessee, he said, "Boney, they've found 'em! Goddamn, those silly Turners came up with 'em!" Eyes blazing, hitting me on the arm.

"You're kiddin'. How do you know for sure?"

"I done seen one!"

Every time the Turners' mom and dad went out—to church, to visit relatives, anywhere—the Turner brothers, Rufus and Wahoo, flew through the house like burglars, looking for the dirty films they knew their father had secreted someplace. They crawled into recesses of the basement, picked the locks of trunks, lifted mattresses. But for years they had turned up nothing. And Wahoo, the younger one who liked to jiggle his removable front plate in people's faces, only recently began thinking it might have been a dream when he had spied, through a crack in a door and a haze of smoke, his pop screening them once after lights out. "Where did they find 'em?"

"They found 'em," laughing uncontrollably now, near hysteria, "in the living room, right in plain view on the book shelves. They'd been there all the time."

The hysteria was catching. We both put hands on each other's shoulders, breaking away now and then to light-heartedly pop the other's arm. "Which one of the Turners was it?"

"Wahoo." Somehow this was the funniest bit of news yet. I could picture Wahoo's plate going in and out over the cache, and tears popped from my eyes. The laughter was the same nervous variety that hit us in class occasionally when something totally outrageous and unexpected happened—like a backhanded fart from someone at the blackboard. That was how much under wraps we were usually. "Old Wahoo," the Sheik went on, hugging the apple tree now, "I don't think the dopey bastard can read or write. Did you know that?"

"When are they going to show 'em?" getting matters at hand back abruptly.

"They're showing 'em *right now!* Come on, Boney, I only broke away long enough to let you in on this. I know how cunt crazy you are."

Boy, there was a buddy for you. "Listen, go on back up there, and I'll follow you in a few minutes. I got to finish supper."

"Make it snappy, I'm warning you. Their folks only stepped out for an hour or two, and you know what a mean bastard old man Turner is. Their sister Marge might bust in any minute, too." Marge was darkly pretty, energetic, and wore high heels to her classes at the business college. The Sheik couldn't resist tarrying a moment longer to comment: "Boy, I'd sure love to fuck Marge, wouldn't you, Boney?"

93

"Ummm, man."

And then he flew back up the vacant lot. In the dim twilight I could see the speck of him on the Turners' front porch, and then he was passed inside. It must be true! The shades were all drawn in the house, and someone was posted as sentry at the front door. I rushed to finish the pile of beans on my plate with the beaten steak to the side, feeling a marvelous scent of evil leaving the Turners' and wafting now through our windows. If it wasn't evil, then it wouldn't be any good. Temptation, the juice of life, never beckoned from the Central Baptist church; it was the other way around. I could hardly wait to give in. "Chew your food, Johnny," my mother said.

Swallowing the last hunk of meat, chair back, visualizing Fred Astaire putting it to Ginger Rogers in the buff while both danced to "Rio Rita"—would it be like that?—I heard the beep of Uncle Buford's V-8 out front. Pancho beckoned for me to hop in, taking for granted that nothing in life could ever equal car riding. Hands on the window, I told of the Turner brothers' breakthrough. "Come on with me."

"Don't do it, Boney." He had just washed his face, his hair wetly combed. I pictured the way he looked with Meredith, *me* with Meredith. "I'm not going to do it."

"Why?"

"Awww, there're better things to do. Jump in. I've only got the car for a few minutes. . . ." I kicked the ground, squeezing the car door. He pinched his upper lip in that way he had, laughing for a split second like his old self. His new stance was the most pious any of us had—outside of religious saints such as Fruitcake Trammel who, on fear of the devil getting him, wouldn't darken a picture show, read the comic strips, or allow his lips to touch a girl's (until marriage and then only at baby-making time, or so he preached). Now that Pancho had committed himself to something, he went into it, as always, with all his might. This total dedication of his is one way to explain those later crazy events that took the town by surprise. "Hop in. We'll drive by the Pine Crest Addition."

That did it. If I turned down the offer, I was denying Meredith. He would certainly have the lead then because he was paying more attention to her and living up to her ideals. Also, if we drove by her house I might glean from his attitude how well he was in with her. Hopefully, too, there would still be time for me to give in to temptation. I got in.

Driving past the stucco-and-brick home, Pancho slowed to a crawl—head leaning over the steering wheel, looking around me. "She said she was going to study for that English quiz tomorrow. Whoever studies for Miss Godsey? If I see she's gone out, I'll really get to razz her. . . ."

Still playing as if he was just interested in teasing her. . . . Out of consideration to me? "If she said she was going to study, she'll study," I said. How cute Meredith was, thinking she had to memorize those interminable pages of Shakespeare. Her fine morals. The rest of us were copying those quotations on quiz days from open texts in our laps. You'd go balmy otherwise.

There were the two Chevvies her family owned in the driveway. Lights shone upstairs and down, and vague forms moved fleetingly past windows. "She's in. I think I'll give a beep now to scare shit out of her."

He pressed three loud toots on the horn, shattering the country silence, and I sunk deeper in my seat. That wasn't my kind of humor. Dropped off back home, I made as if to go in my house and then, feeling quivers shake me, cut up the vacant lot for the Turners. Mr. Turner, a man who kept a cigarette going nearly always in the corner of his mouth, met me at the door. Squinting from smoke curling around his nostrils and into his eyes, he said the gang could be found down at the Buffalo. He seemed amused. At the poolroom I found out from the Sheik that he hadn't actually caught them with the films, but had discovered that his 8mm Bell and Howell was hot from running. He had hid the films for real after that. "Boney," chalking his cue, while I beat my head with mine till stars flew, "I warned you to hurry. Pancho must be a Grade-A asshole to keep you away. You'd have loved 'em more than anybody. A grocery boy fucks this beautiful housewife right on her kitchen table."

I screamed. "You're lying, Sheik!"

"Ask Wahoo. Everybody. I don't know what's got into Pancho."

And next came the "beer" business. The Sheik had stolen four quarts of Ballantine from his father's restaurant, had hidden them for awhile in the far reaches of my basement, and then had let the word out in the neighborhood that they'd be drained Saturday night in the vacant lot. The football season was nearing an end, our team hadn't beaten anyone, it was time for some kind of celebration. We sat in pale moonlight on the grass until our butts got too cold, then stood, passing a brown quart from hand to hand, refraining, in a show of comradeship, from wiping the bottle after it had just left a friend's lips. It tasted like soap, and it was all I could do to get down a few swallows. What I dearly wanted was the excuse to warble "Down by the Old Mill Stream," throw my arms around my buddies, maybe yell *Fuck Everybody,* and then pass out. I'd get some respect at school after that. While I waited for the chance, Pancho came up—hands deep in pockets, hunching up, staying a little outside the circle. The Sheik had the bottle then and he held it toward him. "Take some."

"You know I don't drink, Sheik."

"You're afraid to. You ain't got the guts. That's the reason."

"Yeah, sure, Sheik." He watched the Sheik then take a mighty pull, two gurgles puffing up, the Sheik's little finger extended as it was when shifting gears or aiming a cue. It did look funny. "Look at the fat boy go. He, he."

"That does it. The real true reason you don't drink is because your old man is a drunk and flew the coop."

Pancho came out of his hunch, hands from pockets, fists doubled-up. In the moonlight his face seemed drained of color. None of us had quite seen anger like this before. Once Tuffie Brown, when called "Trash" (his family lived in a ramshackle house, father out of work) by Rufus Turner, had choked Rufus a light purple before being pried apart, but that was as close to Pancho's anger as we had seen. He was trembling, lips quivering. "Ghazi, you . . ."

"Aw, take it easy. I was just kiddin'."

". . . *son of a bitch.*"

Now the Sheik was just as angry. Maybe it was the way Pancho enunciated the words, giving it a literal ring. The Sheik's mother was dead, we all remembered. We then had to leap on both their shoulders, holding them down for the longest time, sweet-talking them for hours—the beer forgotten. Surely they'd be mortal enemies after this. A few days later, in fact, they made up over a game of pool, Pancho winning. It could have been that after such fierce anger it was almost a sensual delight to make up. Or it was that each was drawn closer now that both knew they carried common, unspeakable wounds. Buddies again—but each never forgetting that moment of truth.

So while the Sheik and Pancho carried the football team through its last gasps, I went out, while no one was looking, for the basketball team. Coach B. B. Baker was a short man, gray hair sliced down the middle, with a shiny, unlined and tanned face that set off clear, blue eyes. He went for long stretches without speaking, chin raised, reflective, almost seeming ready to burst from wisdom. The motley crew before him—rejects mostly from the football squad—warmed up with favorite, untaught shots and a little dribbling against each other. The sound echoed delightfully through the vacant gym, the strong smell of past contests hanging in the air. Suddenly, a tweet from Coach Baker's whistle, and he would walk up in the slow, calculated stride of a policeman in search of a crime, trickily wrenching a ball out of my hands in a flash without looking at me. Was he showing how easily a ball could be stolen from me? I felt like a fool. His words raced from his mouth in fire-engine speed: "Two lines. Run down court. Two at a time. Toss ball back and forth. Run!" *Tweet!* "Go!"

"How's that, Coach? Could you repeat that one?"

"I want two boys know what I'm talking about! You . . . you. *Go!*"

He blew spit up in the air from his whistle; and gone was the Woodrow Wilson stance. Two boys took off like greased lightning, the ball slung back and forth, no dribbling. Then followed other drills—running around in circles, throwing the ball to someone unsuspecting, crisscrossing in front of each other. Nothing had to do with sinking the ball through the net, what I'd always thought basketball was about. I wore a flaming red sweat suit, having done the messy dyeing at home myself, hoping its brilliance would facilitate Meredith picking me out in case she strolled by. The wartime atmosphere of scarce goods still prevailed and we had to supply our own warm-up equipment and jockstraps. Shoes, though, for a change, were another matter. The school hoarded a stock, like a whiskey supply, in a locked, cavelike vault under one side of the stands. Those shoes, like no other footwear ever, had black leather sides around white rubber soles, and were a mark of distinction to the wearer. After a week of running the court, crisscrossing in front of my buddies, it came to me that I was the tallest there and might make the team. "Coach Baker," I said, cornering him after practice in his office filled with trophies from other coaches' teams, "do you think I might latch onto a pair of those black leather shoes?"

"Why weren't you out for the team last year?" he slung out, surprising me like stealing the ball. "You made a big mistake there. Why oh why weren't you around?"

He marched by, at armpit level, heading for the shoe vault. I followed, watching his more-than-adequate seat move. "I wasn't feeling too hot last year, Coach."

"You need training. Boy, do you need training." He tried one key; it didn't work. He tried two more. He wasn't listening to a thing I said. "Do you live in the country? Have a barn around you?"

"There's this old broken-down ba—"

"I want you to jump. Jump up and touch the barn rafters. If one's not around, I want you jumping up to touch tree branches. Keep extending yourself and touching things you couldn't touch a week before. Get me?"

"Got you, Coach!"

Inside the vault he shot forward, and, following the direction of his behind, I suddenly felt as if a blackjack had cracked my skull. Everything went white, my knees gave, and a brutal pain charged from my head down my neck. Ever since reaching my new height I had been bumping into things, but never a low concrete ledge at such a tilt. I passed out a second and then followed the sound of Coach Baker's pep talk to where he stood holding a shoe box, ". . . I've always given preference to boys who are prepared. Try this on for size."

My face screwed up in agony, trying to tell him what the matter was, I finally pulled on a shoe. "My head, ooh, ooh. . . ."

He still wasn't listening. "Now if I let you use those shoes, you promise me you'll jump up and touch things at home?"

"Ooh, yes, sir. Ooh, I promise."

Coach Baker was himself a reject. His first season was always glory-filled, with the material some other coach had already developed. And then the next year on his own—using his own peculiar methods and grooming players himself—would be a disaster. After a couple of seasons like that he would move on to fiddle again with what a more successful coach had left behind; and in his nomadic career somehow always moved up the ladder instead of down. He *looked* like a coach—chiseled tanned features, iron-gray hair, school sweat shirt with a whistle around his neck—and he was continually brought in on a job in a great burst of enthusiasm, by eternally optimistic athletic boards mesmerized by those spectacular winning seasons. The prior season Coach Baker's team, composed of maniacs trained previously by someone else, had almost won the state championship. This year—*my* season—was the first with his own material and methods. The shoe fit, and I wondered which star on the famous near-championship team had worn them.

The day before our first game Coach Baker tweeted his whistle, bounced the ball a couple of times, and then pointed first to one, then another, fielding a team of five. He did not say they would be the starting group, saving that for a more dramatic moment, but just shoved the ball our way and let us move it around at one end of the court. I was included, at the position of center. *Starting!* The magic of that word—one chosen among many, given a slice of glory no matter what happened in the game. The ball felt different now, a piece of imitation leather I had the full right to handle and sling. I shot with authority, taking on a look of gravity that befitted someone selected for such an important assignment. Could I possibly wait for tomorrow night—the band playing, Meredith Lancaster leading the cheers in maroon satin panties, dribbling out on the court to warm up?

The night of the game I had my mother cook me an early supper, could only peck at it, and then spent two hours in anguish waiting for a decent moment to stroll to the school gym. I didn't want to get there way ahead of everybody else, leaving myself open to ridicule. This was one time I needed no laughs. I listened to the radio, Bing Crosby warbling "Swinging on a Star," barricaded myself in my room and, shades tight, shot a few practice hooks over my head in a tricky, unique style I had invented. Being exhausted, I tried to nap, but unsuccessfully. I read the paper over and over, returning to the two-paragraph item that told of our upcoming game. It was like those Christmas Eves of long before when I would be gritting my teeth an hour before dawn, waiting to get at those presents.

And then the clock finally said time to go. Out into the dark street, down the hill and over the path by the Negro shanty, up to the gym entrance where Mr. DePew sat enthroned at the ticket window. I shot him a glance and a nod and he returned it, signifying he knew my status and that I wasn't to fork over twenty-five cents to be admitted. I was on the team. We dressed in a funeral-like stillness, hearing the muted rumble of the stands beginning to fill above us. Then we stood in line, shivering a little from drafts, waiting for the B Team—composed of shorties whom we barely deigned to acknowledge—to finish their pointless encounter. Finally, the last whistle for the preliminaries came and we set sail down court in a flurry of dribbling, the band upstairs unleashing

"Fight, Wildcats, Fight!," the cheerleaders twirling, clapping, screaming. We hadn't even started yet, but what a warm-up we gave them: full of the tricky, crisscrossing patterns Coach Baker had shown us and inventive, peculiar shots we had thought up on our own. If everything could have stopped right there, the game forgotten, it would have suited me. But into the shoe vault we went, to get final instructions from Coach Baker—giving only the tiniest glance to the strange aggregate at the other end of the court, our enemies.

Coach Baker's cheeks had turned florid, and he couldn't stand still. The rest of us sat on cold benches, winded from the warm-up. We wore the satin drawers, voluminous on most of us, that the near-champions had sported the year before. But that heroic bunch, at the end of the season, had claimed their silky, numeraled jerseys as keepsakes, leaving our team now, in the continuing wartime bereftness, decked out in white BVD undershirts with homemade numbers sewn on. "Everyone gets one of these, though I would advise chewing only half," Coach Baker said, handing out sticks of gum. Was this in the athletic budget or had he bought them on his own? He was chewing up a storm himself. "Chew. It'll help steady you down. . . ." He barked out the starting five, those of us who had been slinging the ball together and knew our status already, giving it a tense, Knute Rockne ring. "Now don't think that because you're playing country boys out there tonight that this is going to be a pushover. All they do out there at that country school is *play* basketball anyhow. But you can win, this team can go all the way to the championships if it wants to. . . ."

We waited, on the edge of the cold bench. We waited for strategy, what our moves should be, the final word. "All right," throwing open the shoe-vault door, to the glistening court outside, "GO GET ON THEM BIRDS!"

We stood in a growl and raced. And I did it again: Right into the low concrete ledge, reeling back almost unconscious. My vision came back sharply when I pumped the hamlike hand of the boy (or man) playing against me. He had that distinctive smell of the barnyard to him, thick curly hair, and a five o'clock shadow. He smiled awkwardly, proud, I imagined, that he was playing in the city. After all, our school had claimed a near-championship the year before. And I wasn't going to let down sophisticated city ballplaying either! A cheer, and the ref—a tall man who walked as if his back was killing him—held the ball up, whistle poised. He had dressed silently in the locker room with us, his rear decorously turned to cut off any view of a referee-type wang, guarding any familiarity or show of preference. I sort of said hello, but he didn't acknowledge it. A game was deadly serious, no time for pleasantries. The whistle, the ball up in the air, and everything passed slowly as if in a dream. . . .

That night, after it was over, as I lay in bed, muscles still jumping, I played and replayed each decisive moment until finally the morning paper plopped on the front porch with its write-up. There was that first moment under the board when the ball had miraculously ended up in my hands and I did a lay-up. God, it had actually counted; I saw the points go up on the mechanical scoreboard. But there were bad moments, too. I had heard someone distinctly catcall from the stands: "Give Boney a transfusion, he looks like he's been locked up in a brickyard furnace!" I'd love to get whoever that was. And the country boy had been dangerous in his awkwardness, an elbow catching me in the Adam's apple, a scratch down the side of my cheek, stepping on my foot. The referee, though, called me for a foul in grazing a wrist, and when I said, "What's up, sir?" slapped on a technical. No talking to the ref.

Some nonplaying moments had been great: during time-outs to look sideways up in the stands. My father up there somewhere, lunch pail in hand, off to work his trick after the battle. And when I was taken out for a breather, near the half, Meredith came up with a worried frown: "Oh, you've been hurt, there's blood running down your face," as if a dueling saber had creased there. It was only where the country boy had dislodged a pimple, but I dabbed with a towel, turned speechless, and noted how her breasts looked bigger as she leaned over. Somehow we won. With no game plan other than the crisscrossing warm-up, we made blind, over-the-head hooks, shots on the dead run, and once someone heaved a two-pointer from up between his legs at mid-court. The charms of the near-championship team still worked—and we whooped it up in the shower room, the ref taking a private stall to himself, Coach Baker shaking his head and nearly smiling. And that morning edition of the paper listed all our names, mine in the center of the starting five, having good words for us all and predicting another great year on the hardwood. Perhaps a real championship this time.

For a few days there was that distinct tingle of glory won. Men who had once played the game before screaming fans sought you out, giving advice or just smiling to let you know you were now a member of their fraternity. The Sheik cornered me, talking solely of basketball, although he couldn't play the game, beaming when others passed to confirm his right to some reflected glow. Pancho remained aloof, but I thought I understood. Unless he was involved in a game himself, its trappings left him cold. I pictured carrying the season on till I was about eighty years old, Meredith cheerleading at time-outs, coming up with worried frowns at injury-breaks, eventually going with me for Cokes and bar-be-cues after the game the way the big couples did it.

But tingles of glory are always brief, and before we played our next home-court game, the football season had ended and several of the brutes let loose from the squad now came out for basketball. They had larger, seemingly more hairy calves, rougher ways under the boards, and a sort of reckless good humor. They crisscrossed for Coach Baker, hooting and bumping each other, roughhousing and tripping an opponent in pursuit of the ball. Probably after the hard-nosed demands of football and constant losses, it seemed like a holiday now to run around in sneakers and biff someone in a heated room. They acted superior. Pancho was among them. And after my position.

"All right, you football boys," Coach Baker said, tweeting first, all balls stilled from bouncing, "I want to tell you that you have a lot of catching up to do. These other boys," waving my way, "have been giving it all they got for the last month. You're just not going to come in here and take over. You got that clear?" The football boys smiled, still on holiday. The football coach used to strike them with his fist and kick them in the ass. "O.K.," tweet, "let's see some scrimmage!"

Under the boards Pancho sank an elbow into my belly as we went up, enough to allow him to come down with the ball. Trotting up court, I said, "You're playing dirty, goddamnit."

"I know," chortling, like old times. How could you get mad at your old buddy?

And he was a terrible shot. Surely Coach Baker, whistle flapping, could see that. He needed to be but inches away from the hoop before he could sink one, sending the ball into the stands on the long set shots. But he did look good on court, muscles and veins bulging, black hair flying. My dyed-red sweat suit was no match for his flair.

The next game started out familiarly, the band tooting as we dribbled out for our spectacular, crisscrossing warm-up; then into the shoe vault where we sat while Coach Baker paced before dealing out the gum. And I was learning: Hold back some of your excitement and energy so you can use it in the last part of the game. I hadn't quite torn the breath out of myself on warming up this time. And when Coach Baker called my name for the starting five, I nodded as if there would never be any doubt. He peeked out the door, came back in a flush to touch all our hands in a cluster, and said, "O.K. GO GET ON THEM BIRDS!"

For once I didn't crack my head, flying out in a Groucho Marx crouch. And at mid-court, in the center's spot, my opponent waited in a sort of crouch himself, hands on knees for the jump, a sneaky smile—like that of a magic potato-peeler salesman—on his face. But, again, a country boy—probably awkward. That too pleasant smile was the only thing that gave me pause. Up went the ball from the stiff-backed ref, and one of our guards came up with it. At our end of the court, I did a fake here, a fake there, something like a hot-cha dance step, and all at once felt the ball sail into my hands. As if taken spastic, I threw myself into the twisting, over-the-head and behind-the-back shot I loved to do in the warm-up to band music. The son of a bitch went in—a cheer stabbing the air. I trotted up court, flicking my head to see the two points go up, flicking back to see Meredith's satin-covered behind on a cheerleader leap. Boy, tonight I'm going to conquer sports!

We took our stances now at their end of the court, everything growing still in the stands. Near the basket the country boy got in his crouch, hands on knees, and I stood behind him waving my arms. I noticed by its scent that he used Vaseline hair tonic, my brand. Here came their sawed-off guard, dribbling to the side for what looked like a shot. No—as if they had real, thought-out plays on this team—he side-armed the ball to the boy in front of me. Up in the air I went, arms like windmills. The ball shot back to the guard, and he then peeled off down the center lane in an arc while the country boy put his leg and hip in my way, elbows out a mile. That guard turned into a five-foot blur, his white knee guards pumping, as he tore in for the lay-up, no one near him. *Who was supposed to get him!* The country boy looked over his shoulder at me in that magic potato-peeler salesman of a smile.

We lost the ball at our end of the court—they took it away from us, in fact—and once more that five-foot vision side-armed the ball to the country boy who ricocheted it back while easing a hip and elbow into me. I could see them working on this play in their country-style gym that probably had rickety stands for about twenty-five. We were from the hub-city of upper east Tennessee, near-champions of yester-year; how could they pull this fancy stuff on us? Again, that guard sailed by at stomach-level for the lay-up. At our end I dribbled to the far side, near the black out-of-bounds mark, and, pretending I had some strategy going, heaved one blindly and furiously, hearing from the stands as the ball departed, "Don't shoot, idiot!" It went through, not touching the rim. They came back at us with other, well-coordinated plays, all seeming to involve the country boy's hip in my way. The feel of his flesh was hairy and slightly cool; he wasn't even working up a sweat. We called time-out, arguing till our breaths gave out over who was responsible for the flying guard. We tried our impossible shots that had worked so well the game before, making enough to keep the stands screaming, but the other team came back like clockwork with those well-coordinated maneuvers. They moved steadily ahead. And, halfway through the second quarter, I looked up from a time-out to see Pancho come trotting in with his hand raised. I was going out.

Rubbing a towel over my face on the bench, I saw Coach Baker coming my way. He'd probably congratulate me on those points I'd sunk—about half the team's score—or tell me to get my rest for the second half. Then we'd solve the puzzle. He said, "You let that bird block you." He wheeled. "GET ON 'EM, PANCHO!"

Pancho started the second half. Now, under the boards, the elbows and knees really flew, the ref's whistle in an almost constant tweet. The ball—when it did go in now—was usually powered by several hands, like the marine aggregate raising the flag on Iwo. In the final two minutes Pancho fouled-out—but by then we were leading. I had time enough to go in and pass once from behind my back—to a whoop from the stands—and sink a one-arm push shot from out of nowhere. The country boy wasn't moving too fast now. In the locker room, winners, Pancho chortled. "You see me take care of that bozo? I got him in the nuts where he lives." The paper the next day praised our character in being able to come from behind to win, again prophesying a championship.

At practice Monday, after the crisscrossing, Coach Baker called for the ball. "O.K., I want these five boys down at that end. I want them to pass the ball around and get the feel of working together." I knew, before he called one name. Down at that hallowed end, reserved for the starting five, Pancho now moved. That was Coach Baker's way of telling me I had been replaced. Now in my jaunty red suit I slung the ball around at the other end with boys who were too heavy or too awkward or too carefree for a regular spot. In time we scrimmaged against the chosen five, making jokes among ourselves and passing time. The Chosen carried serious miens—as I had once done, as Pancho now did. In the shower, steam billowing through the cold drafts, Pancho said, "Boney, you just let me elbow you out. I played dirty on you."

"Aw, naw," resignedly, fate will out, "you'll probably play better'n me."

We lost the next game, although it certainly wasn't Pancho's fault. We took on the mighty Kingstown Tigers, featuring this season a 250-pound ex-football lineman at center. On the gridiron his opening trick was to toss sand in the eyes of an opponent. Now—the ref's back turned—he slugged left and right, furious to near insanity if someone did it to him, explosive at the world's injustice if the ref caught him out of the corner of his eye. And, in time, the ref seemed leery of calling fouls on him. Face blazing like Coach Baker's, he seemed capable of murder—if not on court, then catching you some night on a dark street. East Tennessee's most outstanding loser, he was the model of a gentleman in victory. He trotted into our dressing room at the close, shaking everyone's hand, even that of Coach Baker who was in shock, saying, "Fine game, there. Fine, fine." Even giving my mitt a squeeze, although I hadn't gone in. The paper the next day told us to cheer up, we'd just had an off-night. The season hadn't really begun. We could still catch that illusive championship.

The truth was, we didn't win another game. Not one. But the full measure of a totally disastrous season did not come all at once; it came in small, odd dosages. Several of us—the subs—began missing practice, or cutting-up when there. What did it matter? One chubby boy with a fine row of teeth, a sub on last year's near-champions, completely lost heart. He had so looked forward to waddling up and down court, flashing his teeth at the grandstand, and now look at what had happened. One game, after Coach Baker had called the Starting

Five with his name absent once more, he trotted from the shoe vault to up in the stands himself, silky drawers, numeraled BVD undershirt and all. He refused to sit on the bench any longer.

We lost to great, important teams; we lost to some of the most obscure in the state. One school carried the colors of an unincorporated community that served mainly as a way station for the U.S. mail. Its team came out with seven members —five to start, two dwarfs for emergencies, all in what looked like their underwear. They had no band, no cheerleaders, a court with loose boards to trip over and goals with torn, grimy nets. We dressed in a classroom with scarred desks, for they had no locker rooms. And they beat us, playing far over their heads, we were told, for the honor of knocking off a Big City team that had once sported near-champions. On the bus ride back to our school and a shower, I pulled the cord near my block, getting a laugh. "Who did that?" Coach Baker screamed, to no answer. "Nobody's getting off. We're all in this together!"

Finally, although he still called for the crisscrossing maneuvers, gave out gum, and screamed, "GET ON THEM BIRDS," the spark dimmed in Coach Baker's blue eyes. Once more the usual: Grooming his own material, he had lost. He must have felt like the skipper of a continually sinking ship, having to hold to the rituals of the bridge as he watched the bow go under again. It came to me, catching his burnt-out expression once on the bench, that maybe he didn't really know how to play the game. One game he screamed, "Why's the ref stopping it?"

"Why, Coach," someone explained, "it was a double-dribble."

"Oh."

But no matter what the outcome—a near victory or a

massacre—Pancho played well, bringing in a well-timed elbow, a fist, letting the other team at least know they had been in a physical contest. And he was out there sixty minutes for all the world, Meredith especially, to see. He started taking her out after games, and a few times *before*. One late afternoon, trying in vain to catch a snooze, hoping I might be called upon to play a minute or two that night, I heard him yell. "Hey, Boney, gettin' your rest for the game?"

I started to jab my middle finger upward from behind the bed's headboard, thought better, and peered around the bedpost—quickly withdrawing. There he was with Meredith, cupping a weed in his hand, while she carried an armload of books at chest level. My heart sank. They were headed for Uncle Buford's . . . but for *what?* To smooch in the living room, sneak up to Pancho's athletic-smelling room? I had stopped asking Pancho questions about Meredith by now, afraid that if I kept showing interest he wouldn't tell me a thing. He was that way. He had to volunteer tidbits, and—after waiting long enough—he did so.

"Boney," one night on the front walk, before my home, "I rubbed Meredith's stomach the other night."

"Yeah," feeling faint.

"She asked me to. Yeah," chortling, like giving someone the elbow, "she said it was hurting her down there. I started high up, but she kept saying, 'Not there, not there. Lower.' " He demonstrated, in a circular motion, how he did it. "Girls have this stomach thing, you know. It hurts them every so often."

"Yeah." I should have bitten my tongue. "Then what happened?"

"Oh, ho, ho, wouldn't you like to know."

It was left to my imagination—which was where most of my information on girls came from anyhow. One early morning in study hall Meredith took the seat behind me. All right, I told myself, you simply have to talk to her now that you have this chance. Turning, close to her face, I whiffed a sharp bouquet that must have come from her breath, and there was a pimple, unsuccessfully covered by powder, on the side of her chin. *No!* It can't be! I jabbered to others around her, wanting to guard her, keep the innocent from discovering these imperfections, telling myself my eyes and nose had lied. Reality had to be fought on all fronts, but caught you unawares when you least expected it.

That Saturday started off quite ordinarily in the Buffalo. A sliver or two of sunlight broke through the cracked and smoky windows at the front. The Sheik ate three hot dogs with onions, asked if anybody was getting any pussy, and lost a game of snooker when he spotted someone twenty points. Ernie Peoples shot past outside, swiveling his neck for a quick look-see in the hellhole. Pancho beat a fish at nine ball, a brickyard worker in overalls covered with a reddish dust, a chaw in the side of his mouth. Money must have come hard for the man, and I didn't want to stand around to watch the slaughter.

I was fooling around with a rack of balls on the straight table when Humphrey Pernell eased up. His real name was not Humphrey, but we called him that because, even at sixteen, he greatly resembled Humphrey Bogart—right down to his five o'clock shadow, long upper lip, and high forehead. He'd even taken to leaving a butt in the corner of his mouth, smoke curling up into large watery eyes.

But a greater claim to distinction than his resemblance to the actor was his reputation as the meanest boy in town. All parents—when they were in residence themselves—warned against bringing him home. He tracked in mud, stole knick-knacks that weren't nailed down, and brought up subjects like farts when women were around. His pure meanness was almost ennobling. Once during a tense game of straight—one hundred dollars a go-round, all other tables shut down for the match—Humphrey had marched by Floyd Waters, the town's leading gambler and thug, who was carefully aiming through manicured fingers at a decisive ball, and goosed him. Goosed Floyd Waters who wore silk shirts, sharply creased twill trousers without back pockets, and alligator shoes. Goosed someone who flew every year to the Kentucky Derby. And said, "Check your oil, pretty boy?"

Floyd Waters had miscued on the one-hundred-dollar shot, and then had chased Humphrey down Main Street, swinging the loaded end of his cue at his head, but only grazing him. Humphrey was mean and lucky. Now he was beside me, the corner of his upper lip lifting for speech. "They got some new girls down at the Dixie, I hear. You game for some poon tang?"

It was as if I'd been waiting for this moment all my life. I said, "Er, would you make the arrangements?"

"Natch. How much folding you carrying?"

"Nine." I had eleven.

"Good. You can loan me two, I'm a little short."

At the Dixie the black porter, LeRoy, stood as always with his back lightly resting on the plate glass, a highly soiled bellhop's cap down on his forehead. No one ever brought luggage into the Dixie, but, if they did, it would be doubtful if LeRoy could lift it. His function, as our legends had it, lay elsewhere. Humphrey eased beside him, as he had to me. "Don't lie to me, now. What do these new girls you got look like?"

LeRoy's head faced one way down Market, his walleye

coming back the other at Humphrey. It was a little eerie. "They young."

"How much for a crack at 'em?"

"You pay them. Five, I reckon."

"O.K., let us at 'em."

"Wait." LeRoy dislodged himself from the plate glass, causing it to rattle. "You got to register first."

An edge of panic rose. Register? I wanted to back out, but Humphrey was already diving into the Dixie's dimness. I peered up and down Market, on the outlook for my father, then tiptoed in behind. Past potted plants, broken down armchairs and rockers, a spittoon or two. Far back at a cubicle a stooped, frail man held open a register, a pen uplifted. "It's a buck per," he said, tiredly, hardly noticing us. How could he be so calm? My teeth were chattering.

"Aw, buddy, pretend you don't see us," Humphrey said. "We're going to be in and out quick."

"Hit's the rules."

"O.K., Boney, pay him."

Now that I was past the gates, having fought past the initial barrier, nothing was going to stop me. I handed over two singles, and then signed our high school principal's name on the dotted line. Each step creaked in turn as we followed LeRoy up the stairs. The hall that faced us upstairs had an unshaded light hanging down, a warped floor covered by cracked linoleum. After all this time, can it be true? After all the yarns, pictures, daydreams—is it now going to happen? LeRoy knocked on a door that showed streaks of light escaping from the bottom. "Come in, it ain't locked," a hard and weary female voice called.

There were two of them inside. A brunette sat hunched forward on a straight chair, legs crossed, her chin resting in her palm. She was dressed just like women you see walking every day down on Main Street. But the blonde, stretched out on the bed, wore a gauze-thin gown that I'd never seen anybody in my life wear. One hand lay across her stomach, the other playing with a loose thread in the bed cover. She seemed the boss. "These boys old enough, LeRoy? You know 'em?"

"I know 'em, they all right."

After LeRoy vanished in a welter of smiles, head cocked to the side, someone now had to make a move. Humphrey, despite all his bragging and the actual bravery shown in goosing Floyd Waters, turned to stone. A corner of his mouth was frozen in a Humphrey Bogart grin, hands locked in his pockets. "I'll take her," I said, moving beside the blonde on the bed.

"O.K.," the brunette whined, "I'll take you'ern buddy into the next room."

Now, after first having to slip Humphrey two dollars, palm down so as to hide it, I was alone with the blonde. She still lay there quietly, fooling with that loose thread. *Her* five dollars I put on a scarred and wobbly bureau which she nodded toward. Now what? The shade was all the way up on the lone window, a thin curtain, thinner than the blonde's gown, waving back in the breeze. Outside I saw people walking on Market Street, acting as if it was just any old day. There went Mr. St. John, hobbling on his Jake leg, a stiff-legged affliction caused by drinking a certain type of bootleg liquor during the 1920's. Quite a few men—some prominent, church deacons naturally—swung a Jake leg around town, an embarrassment to their families.

Down to my shorts, and not a patched pair I was happy to note, I positioned myself beside the blonde. Since I'd forked over the money, I felt I now had certain rights. I played with her breasts, jiggling them up and down, hurriedly because I didn't know how much time was allotted there. A slight clawing at the frilly strap of the gown, and one breast popped out in the clear. It was big, with a dollar-sized nipple. I didn't want her to think I was sissy or perverted, so I held myself back from kissing it. Then, like folding over a sheet, I raised back the skirt of her gown. And there before my eyes it was, much darker than her regular hair had led me to believe. Might as well play a little down here, too, while I got the chance. All girls had one: teachers who were sexy, moving picture actresses, Meredith. She parted her legs, seeming to think I knew what I was doing. I patted it like a mud pie.

"Come on. Get out of them shorts. Want to use anything?"

I nodded, and handed over a condom Humphrey had let me have; share and share alike. My back to her, shorts dropped (Lord, don't let my dad or someone like Mr. DePew pass on Market Street), I threw a fantasy or two into the hopper, willing myself to get bigger. No such luck; the opposite. My teeth were chattering. "They turn off the heat in here?"

"They either roast you or freeze you around here. Here now," she said, touching where all my thoughts were now racing. She didn't seem to think it wouldn't do the job, didn't seem to be thinking much about it at all. She took it between fingers and thumb, as if it was some sort of flower, working it up and down while she brought the condom down with the other hand. Get hard, I willed, shivering stopped and sweat starting. Twenty-three hours out of the day you won't go down, and now look at you. I began playing with her breasts because I didn't know what else to do. It rose suddenly, almost flew up in urgency, when I stopped thinking about it. But, wait, isn't there a certain way to connect—like the proper way to bridge a cue or shoot a foul? I rolled over on her anyhow, bluffing. "Now don't tell me," she said, "that you don't know how to screw?"

"I do, I do!"

"Then hold yourself off till I draw my knees up. Like this." My arms were killing me from that push-up position. "Come down now. Right here in the center. Easy. Hold on." She spat in her hand, reached down to wet the sheath—and I felt the juices, oh God, begin their throb of escape. No time to lose now, no more time for instruction. I went in on the last throb, and battered around in a frenzy until she said, "O.K., you've come. Get off."

Clothes back on in a flash—it didn't seem right to lounge about nude in the middle of the day—I sat on the side of the bed, waiting for Humphrey. A creak of bedsprings could be heard, a long silence, and then a woman's shriek and curse. The brunette swung in ahead of Humphrey, clutching her purse in front of her. "That 'un," she said, nodding back over her shoulder, "I caught trying to steal his 'ere money back."

"Oh, you just got a wild hair," Humphrey said, chuckling, his old self now. "I was looking for a weed. Gimme a smoke, will ya, Blondie, I just run out." He took a Luckie from a bedside table, faked on inhaling, and then sat in a chair facing her and me. "Did he have a big enough wing-wang on him, baby?"

"Yes." I loved that blonde.

"Why don't we switch? Do one on the house for us? Nobody'd know, and you'd never forget the way I throw the pipe."

"I'm sure. Come up with some more money, and we will."

Humphrey dropped the subject. He asked where they came from. The blonde from Detroit; the brunette from the Kentucky hills. He wanted to know how they got in the business. They wouldn't say, looked at their watches. "Well, let's shove, Boney," Humphrey said, standing and then wheeling around to give the blonde—*my* blonde—a big feel right on the snatch. Felt it right there in front of everybody. And laughed. "So long, baby," he said, through a tight-lipped Bogart grin. And we hightailed it out, although the blonde seemed only slightly irritated, not mad.

We returned to the Buffalo, everything looking the same as when we'd left: The dreamy hot-dog girl still dishing them out at the counter, Pancho taking the last bit of change from the brickyard worker. Bringing out some pocket change myself, I set Humphrey up to a game, neither of us really caring who won or lost, both unusually polite and respectful of each other now. It was as if we'd just fought an enormous battle together, in competition then but now tied deeply by the common experience; like Krauts and GI's, savoring the memory of coming through alive at St. Lô. Humphrey even sweet-talked the rack boy, a colored man of about eighty with only two fingers on his right hand, out of a quarter so that he could set me up to one, too.

Now I liked strolling by the Dixie—or *daydreaming* I was strutting by when held back by weather or classes—head high, a wave to LeRoy, wearing an old school sweater of my brother's with a football "letter" on it. I pictured, but was too ashamed to tell anybody, the idea of their giving out "letters" at school for outstanding fucks—and coaches to help us out along the way. Here I saw Mr. DePew, baton in hand, pointing to a couple getting it together on his cleared-off desk. I could hear his high-pitched voice call out quite distinctly: "Now you'll notice how Mary Sue brings her knees up here at a good ninety-degree angle, thus allowing the free-flow piston movement from down below. Look at her take it, class. Every bit of it. Whoowee." I would be on the Starting Five this time. And at the end of the year we'd all have our pictures in the yearbook, the cheerleaders lying back with heads out of sight, maroon skirts raised, identified only by their quims.

I let Pancho know about the afternoon at the Dixie, being

118

at first a little hesitant, and he treated the news in one of his strange ways as I'd suspected he might, in a way like an adult looking down at some of our mischief. He didn't ask specific questions about anatomy, didn't jump up and down. He said I'd better be careful, Humphrey could land me in trouble. The Sheik, however, went to pieces, for I told him the blonde was a dead-ringer for Maria Montez. He rifled the till at the Roxy, and then flew through the formalities at the Dixie without asking questions. That night he cornered me in the vacant lot. "Boney, they must have shipped that blonde out. Guess who I got? Old Janette Randolph who used to be with us in the seventh grade. God, I damn near died when I opened the door and there she was. She weighs a ton."

It was fun now to hang out some with boys who displayed campaign ribbons of their own. And the most decorated in combat, the most battles seen, was Rufus Turner. Having a father who played cards more than he worked, who spent long weekends away at Tennessee football games betting, Rufus began early holding important after-school jobs to bring home the bacon. He had folding money all the time, big enough to pay Wahoo to walk around in his Florsheim shoes for a couple of days, breaking them in, every time he bought a new pair. To me, fascinated by his reputation, he looked like a condom ready for business. His face had a sort of shiny translucent quality, his head coming up from his shoulders in an almost cylindrical shape. Wahoo and I would be sitting on the edge of the mattress in their joint bedroom, watching him prepare for an outing, mesmerized by all his marks of wisdom. "The other night," he related, back to us, dressing in front of the mirror, "I delivered this prescription up to a woman on Chilhowie. She wanted it more than any woman I'd ever seen. But you know something? I just wasn't interested that night. Boys, it happens. Be prepared. Some nights, right out of the blue, you won't want to. No one knows why. But don't let it throw you. It's normal."

In a little dipping motion he wiggled on his standard jock-strap, bringing on his regular shorts over that. He claimed the added protection was necessary because of hard-ons that arose unexpectedly in classrooms and while out in public. Dignity was very important to him. He sometimes changed his shirt three times during a hot day, and his trousers were always neatly creased. After word spread about my foray into the Dixie, Rufus popped up at our door one night unannounced. He sat ramrod straight on the sofa, being quizzed about minuscule matters by my mother and aunt while I squirmed. We'd have to get outside before we could bat the breeze. Rufus poked his nose at some of the books on the shelves, asking questions as if he might be interested. "I certainly did enjoy *Treasure Island*," he said, pulling the volume out, sticking it back in.

My aunt then unleashed a battery of Robert Louis Stevenson facts, his long illness, his final death on Samoa in the South Seas. Rufus nodded his condom-shaped head in a scholarly way, all dignity. "I'm learning three new words a day," he said abruptly. "Wahoo quizzes me every night before we go to sleep." Everyone said that was fine. Outside at last, under a full moon, he gave me a good-natured poke on the arm, and said, "Wanna fuck something good for a change?"

"How's that?"

"Margaret Moody. She graduated from high school about two years ago, works now up at the hospital as an X-ray technician. . . ."

"Margaret Moody, Margaret Moody," I couldn't believe it. "She has red hair and wears glasses, right? Has red cheeks."

He nodded. "All you have to do is meet her getting off

work at the emergency room. Say you'll be happy to drive her home if she ain't already got a ride. Just that."

"But I haven't got a car. I feel like stealing one."

"Get one of your buddies with a car. She'll go for two—but the guy in front's got to pretend he don't know what's happening in back for awhile."

"Margaret Moody, Margaret Moody. You've been doing it with her yourself. Tell me what happened. Come on."

He had discovered Margaret Moody himself one night by chance, on the outlook for tail as usual, strolling by the emergency entrance toward home while she was strolling out. I could picture everything perfectly while he told it, more vividly even than if it had happened to me. And his philosophy made perfect sense, just the two of us talking, under a full moon, in the center of the vacant lot. All women were dying for it. Just come to the point immediately with them, and say you'd use a rubber if they showed any fright or concern. Of course, you just couldn't barge up to any old woman at the Baptist church—but a girl coming out of the emergency room in nurse's white, a glow to her cheeks, she was fair game. Rufus took her out that first evening—strike immediately, no stalling—in his cousin's Nash that he could sometimes borrow in desperate circumstances. They did it parked on Pine Crest Hill, a couple of blocks from where she lived. They took off all their clothes.

"Weren't you afraid you'd get caught? Golly."

"No, I loved putting her ass up before the window, you want to know the truth. Every time a car passed, I'd kind of raise it up and wave." And other times quickly followed. They did it in the woods, in a rowboat, and in the balcony of the Majestic Theater. Rufus even drove her one weekend to Spruce Pine, N.C., where they actually stayed, like a regular

121

couple, in a hotel. "I made her do it before an open window, too. Standing up and bent over while I went in from behind. We both waved out the window, but I don't know what it is about Spruce Pine. They just went on about their business as if people did that out of open windows all the time over there. . . ."

"Jeminy Christmas. But why are you letting me in on it if she's this hot?"

"I'm getting enough. And you shouldn't be paying good money for it down at the Dixie when there's so much free stuff going around."

I cased the emergency room immediately, and, sure enough, here she came swinging out the door in the evening, normal-looking as could be. Just seeing her ginger hair bounce, the flush to her cheeks, giggling now with some other girls in white, made me nearly collapse on the street. Pancho would not hear of using Uncle Buford's car to take her out. He was seeing more and more of Meredith—and we were talking less and less about girls. The Sheik was definitely interested. But his lust could not quite compensate for his horror of hospital scents and corridors. Perhaps it was having lost his mother in the hospital when he was little, something, but he was not physically able to wait around the gray, alcohol-smelling walls. Ernie Peoples himself was in the hospital, being operated on for his cheerleading injury, and was lost for chauffeur's duty; he had some tales, though, of his own about nurses.

I tried over and over to figure out a way of borrowing a car. A major problem, however, was that I was unable to drive and would have to learn how with the car I borrowed. For years I'd been seeking cars—stealing two—in trying to crack the mystery of car driving. Once I agreed to help out in a grocery store, for hardly any pay, just as long as I could deliver goods in one of the store's miniature Austin trucks. The owner, with a stiff Abraham Lincoln face, handed over the keys, taking for granted I could drive. Who *couldn't* drive these days? Groceries loaded, I jerked and backfired out of the rear lot, finding I was heading down the sidewalk in the baby truck instead of the street and unable to stop. I saw terrified faces loom up, old men and women running surprisingly fast, a newspaper and packages suddenly thrown up in the air. I cut sharply and turned over in a shower of flying lettuce and cans and eggs. The owner came trotting up in his white smock as I climbed out, lesson over. "You can't drive," he screamed, Abraham Lincoln face incredulous. "You took right on off and didn't know a doggone thing about what you were doing!"

Maybe if I hadn't been so ashamed about not knowing how to drive—no car in the family, that stigma—maybe I could have just come right out and asked someone to teach me. But admitting at this late date that I couldn't drive, when everybody else in the world could, was like admitting you didn't know how to screw. I just couldn't do it. And now as I lay on the couch in the living room, imagining my father inexplicably bringing home a Chevvy, buying a brick house with a shower instead of a bathtub, I heard the side door open and got a strong whiff of chicken. This would be Wallace "Gizzard" Ross, a half grade ahead of me, delivering our Sunday chicken. He was much shorter than I was, with slicked-down hair and a smile that broke out in several different directions at once. His family owned the huge produce store downtown, filled to the brim with screeching, clawing, and shitting fowls of all sorts, sending off a bouquet that could be caught for miles around when the wind was right.

Gizzard entered into all aspects of the business, home delivery his specialty, but being able to wring necks and pluck feathers when the occasion called for it. And every chicken you bought from Ross's Produce Mart couldn't be anything but fresh, for their motto was "We never kill a hen until the order comes." Sometimes my mother would be pressed for time, and I would be commissioned to go down and bring back a "fryer, around three pounds." Into then that sea of caged, hysterical birds, where feathers floated in the air like dust and a short runway was cleared for headless animals to careen down. Gizzard might be there then in a rubber, crimson-streaked smock that was too big for him, crooked smile plastered on, a hand jabbing into a cage with each order. He would take the bird by the head, get set, and then swing the torso around in a circle or two until it was separated and took off on its own steam down the runway, blood spurting. Someone else down the assembly line—a brother, cousin, sometimes an old colored man—would pluck the feathers in a flash, and you would be handed the remains in thick brown paper. Like all the stores except the five-and-dime, the Rosses never asked for cash—as if money was a sort of embarrassment. Just every so often a bill would arrive through the mail for all the chicken you'd eaten.

And wouldn't it be wonderful, I thought, in our living room which was clogged with books the way the Produce Mart was with birds, if my father was *in business*. Then we'd have a car, by golly, and all the other fathers would know immediately who he was without my going into a lot of rigmarole. I caught Gizzard by the elbow in the side hall, and guided him to the center of the vacant lot. He had lots of folding money always, and wheels. "Margaret Moody," I said. "Do you want a little?"

He spit between the crevice in his two front teeth, a distinguishing mark some boys had and some didn't, like being able to whistle sharply through your teeth. "I don't get off till after six tonight, Boney."

"That's O.K. She'll still be at the hospital then." I couldn't believe I'd finally found someone. Now what? "You will? You'll come by in your car? Around seven thirty?"

"Sure. I ain't had my ashes hauled in a couple of days," spitting past my left shoulder. "I'm ready."

Was some kind of sex available down at that airplane-hangarlike henhouse? It was hard to think of Gizzard making out in ordinary surroundings. But he was outside on the nose at seven thirty, horn honking. He wore a tie now, hair slicked down more than usual, chewing an odd brand of chewing gum. The smell of chicken went away after I was in the car a moment. We parked down from the spotlit emergency door, scooting down in the seat, waiting. We both trembled. "Somebody's got to go in and catch her before she gets out the door," Gizzard said. "No telling which way she might go, and we might lose her."

"You go. You got on a tie."

"I would, but I better stay in the car in case I have to move it. No, go in and get her and then we're on our way."

Since the one behind the wheel was ultimately in command, I started for the door just as the shift in nurses began. Older girls—*women* often—flashed by me, left and right, in their highly starched white uniforms, their rubber soles squeaking on the tile; most in pairs, some alone, all seeming to hold the maturity of Solomon. And down the corridor I spied her—that hair like cinnamon, glasses, white-stockinged legs whipping. While at my back I suddenly found a team hell-bent on wheeling in a colored man on a stretcher. Poor man, he was holding his stomach in terrible pain, fully dressed except for the absence of shoes, wearing faded rayon socks that showed the outline of bunions. Maybe this was the Lord's way of showing what would happen to me if I kept on lusting after pussy. Well, I can't talk to you now, Lord. Here she came, closer, closer. In the past I had had to apply heavy pressure to myself to ask older people for drugstore, grocery, and errand boy jobs, going through long moments of torture before making the first move. It was that kind of time again. "Margaret," I heard myself pipe, "have you got a lift home?"

She looked me up and down. I was one of the tallest people in town, although still sporting the face of a ten-year-old. She seemed to get the whole picture without my saying another word. Then I felt a little sorry for her. What kind of life was this, having strange boys pop up all the time? But as she tarried, my lust won out as usual. "You got a car?" she said.

"Yeah. Right over there," arms flying about, almost dancing. "It's a pleasant night out this evening, don't you think?"

"Who else is in that car?"

"How ya doing, Margaret," Gizzard said from the driver's throne, letting fly with a short shot from between his teeth. "Hop in and we'll go for a ride and then we'll take you home."

"Who you boys been talking to?"

"Nobody. We've just been goofing around, and thought you might need a lift. We got nothing else to do. Come on."

"There's got to be at least one person you know that might have dated me. Think."

"Rufus Turner."

"O.K." She got in.

The rules said that if a girl gave in to just one boy—and *he* let the word fly—then she was available for all hands at any time. Unfair, but that's the way it was. It was like a tiny rent causing a whole dike to crumble and an onslaught to follow. Margaret sat next to Gizzard in the front while I climbed in the back, scooting down. Gizzard drove with his back ramrod-straight, head riveted toward the road, speechless. Margaret leaned an elbow out the window, lit a cigarette in a quick flick of her wrist, and began chattering as if this was just any old occasion. She asked how the hen business was going. "Working me to death," Gizzard said, in a grunt, sailing us over the railroad tracks and past a bar-be-cue stand.

"Don't we want a Coke or something?" Margaret said.

"Not right chet, I think."

She asked about Gizzard's older brother, who was now in service, saying he was "a handsome old thing." And she called Gizzard by his real name, Wallace, giving him suddenly a more important, manly status. He still couldn't speak well—or was the strain of driving too much?—whipping through the gate of the local college, on the way to the woodsy terrain in back of the squat brick buildings. He pulled slowly off the road between two trees, cut the motor, and then turned to Margaret as if his neck were paralyzed. She was jabbering on about the local college, about some of its chemistry courses which she was taking to help in her work, stopping suddenly to say: "What are we doing here?"

The moon cut through on her profile, gave a slight glint to her hair. She waited for an answer, looking back over her shoulder as if she'd just remembered I was there. Now I was going to say something, I really was. Gizzard might have a car, have folding money, but I was going to show him—*and* me—that I was brave enough, and knowledgeable enough, to somehow get myself inside a girl. I wasn't worrying about Margaret Moody herself right now, we'd get to that later. My arms up on the back of the front seat, looking into her glasses and funny smile, I said, "Come on into the back seat, baby. I want to talk to you."

"Can't we talk from where we are?"

"Aw, shoot. Please. Come on. Only a few minutes."

She babbled on about a dance she'd gone to, a movie she'd seen, how handsome she thought Lon McAllister the actor was. Gizzard, swiveling his stiff neck around, told her to visit me in the back. "I'll just take a snooze up here while you're gone."

"Come on, Margaret," I pleaded. "Please, please. Just for a little while. Come on, you can. O.K. then, Goddamnit," I said, suddenly whacking the back of the seat so that Gizzard's head bounced, "The hell with it." I was sure going to check with Rufus Turner tomorrow, you could count on that. Then she said, ever so softly, "All right, but just for a minute or two. Go to sleep, Wallace."

Now that she was with me in the back—leaning her head against the window, white-stockinged legs imperceptively open—the begging, heartfelt this time, began all over again. I swore to God that I would just put it in once, just once. What was the harm in just letting it go in once? It wasn't really like doing it. Please, please, please. No, I mustn't touch her up there, either. It felt like foam rubber anyhow, making it sort of embarrassing all the way around. And what did I think I was doing, my hand pinned down there between her warm knees? Hadn't I promised we'd talk if she came sat with me? Talk. She seemed angry now, squirming, and I was definitely going to have to check in with Rufus tomorrow. But before I knew it, not really my doing at all, our lips went together and she began a deep kind of breathing that seemed partly a moan. Her mouth spread open, and took in my whole puckered lips in a swallow, moving every which direction. God, what had I unleashed? Somewhere along the line she had taken off her glasses—and now, with that kiss, her knees let go of my hand, springing it upward toward a warm, silken haven. This was

128

nothing like the Dixie Hotel. Snaps were undone here, the starched white skirt went up there, and out she came of pink underwear in an almost frantic wiggle. Her eyes were squeezed shut.

In the soft moonlight it looked like a small lap rug down there, a large tuft of the copper-colored hair shooting up and the whole works giving off a sharp, briny scent that put the henhouse to shame. And when my hand went out of sight down there, it discovered a much larger and demanding mouth than the one that had just sucked in my lips. If I'd ever thought my pecker had given me trouble, had made demands on me that nearly drove me crazy, then just look at this. She had something between her legs that an army wasn't going to take care of easily. And here I'd been feeling a little sorry for her, in the back of my mind, about the way I'd whisked her out of the emergency room, how Gizzard had told her to get in the back. Who was the victim now, who'd worked out this back seat scheme to satisfy nature? "Put something on, put something on," she said, in a hoarse breath. "Hurry!"

"Hold on, hold on. I'm trying to."

I'd positioned a Trojan in my right front pocket, the only object there, like a gun ready for a quick draw. Now in hand and rolling on backward, I aimed what there was of me between my open zipper right at the copper-colored forest, balancing myself on one knee, an elbow on the back seat. I lunged, and she screamed, "Don't!"

"God, what now?"

"You don't have on anything."

"Yes, I do. It went on backward. Feel."

"No, I can't touch down there. It's not right." I guess she thought she was still holding on to some sort of purity if she forewent feeling a dick. "Promise you won't do anything if it breaks. Promise."

"I promise, I promise!"

"All right," she said, bringing me down by the small of my back, "put it in."

"It's already in," I said.

Or it was somewhere, I wasn't absolutely sure where. It could have missed the mark, and been between her bottom and the upholstery; or down *into* the upholstery itself. I might have been fucking the Pontiac, for all I knew. That Trojan was like cast iron. But when my sharp bones began pressing at her middle, it didn't seem to matter whether I was in or out. Her moans turned into a near scream, her nails dug into my back, and she shook me up and down like a rag doll. In the midst of it all I felt the tremor of a throb start in my body, reached down to check on the Trojan, and then regretfully let the juice fly. I'd promised about the Trojan, and I wanted to be a nice guy. But for the longest time it didn't seem as if it would ever end with Margaret. Rubber tossed out to add to other campus landmarks, pecker back in place and trying to forget about it, Margaret still held on and kissed me now and then. Kissing was highly respected in movies, so I guess she figured anything she did with her mouth was all right.

"I'm coming back," Gizzard said, over the rim of the front seat. "Change seats, Boney."

"O.K."

"No," said Margaret, kissing me. "Let him stay back here longer. I'm getting tired of all this changing around."

But I was already disengaging myself from warm, wet legs and a mouth that wouldn't leave me alone. Probably Gizzard wouldn't do any good now, paying for being slow and magnanimous in the beginning, but he was going to have his try. Wouldn't it be something if I'd have come through and he wouldn't? Scooting down now in the front seat, I heard rough words exchanged in the back, an argument, and then a brief, wet pause. I peeked, and witnessed the two of them in a deep kiss—Gizzard's mouth moving as wildly as hers. Where had he learned to kiss like that, working so hard in the hen business? Not one of his plastered-down hairs was out of place. Now their words came muffled over the rim of the front seat. Gizzard was speaking into the hollow of her shoulder, and she was chewing on his ear. I saw his little white butt going up and down, heard Margaret's moans—and then it was over, with his popping up to straighten his tie while she ran her hands up and down his arms. Now she wouldn't leave *him* alone. All three of us crammed into the front seat for the drive back, she sat closer to him than to me, adoringly watching his goofy smile and calling him Wallace. Girls were certainly fickle.

We had Cokes at a drive-in, talking as if we'd done nothing other than whip up and down Main Street. But on the way to Margaret's house, Gizzard silently slipped his arm around her. "Nobody has to walk me to the door," she said, although neither of us was making a move when we drove up in front of her nice brick home. She gave Gizzard a final soul kiss, gave me a poke in the ribs as if I'd let her down, and said, "You get the car often, Wallace?"

"I'll call you, baby."

That goofy, satisfied grin clung to Gizzard as he then took me home. He had the look of a winner. Was it only because he had a car?

The distinctions that fell to us were not always those most sought, but we had to live with them. I was elected treasurer of the Honor Society, a post that went to one supposedly honest, scholarly, and discreet. The Honor Society itself was composed of those chosen for their high grades, nontruancy, and general niceness. The Sheik and Pancho—smokers and never an A or B on report cards except for gym—couldn't get within ten feet of it. Meredith was elected president.

And when the first warm days of spring came our senior year, a flowery, grassy scent wafting in through open windows, the Honor Society decided it was time for a hayride. Not a beer bust or jitterbug blast—but a nice, quiet, wholesome hayride. A preacher would probably lead us in prayer before we jumped in the hay, too. So dislodging myself from among the tall shelves of books in the living room, the heat from the furnace that would stay on until July, I picked up the black phone in the hall, positioned myself once again on the side steps, and called Meredith. Why, yes, yes, she said, in that enthused, out-of-breath voice—I could picture her wide eyes—she'd just love to go on that hayride with me. It took only a few minutes for my heart to quit its wild pumping this time.

For once I didn't need a car. At the back of the school building that balmy spring evening a large farm truck loomed where the principal's decrepit Ford was usually parked, greenish-brown hay piled high between its side slats. Everyone was on his own to get there by taking-off time of seven thirty. Everyone, that is, who had handed over to the treasurer—me —a half a buck. No freeloaders in the Honor Society. "Meredith," I had said, "I'll pay your fifty cents for you."

No, no, she had breathed, in shock. She must donate the money herself. No, really, she must.

And she would get down to the schoolhouse on her own, like everyone else. I stood near the truck, cursing a pimple that had brazenly risen that afternoon on my left cheek after a week's smooth sailing without blemishes, crossing off names as the Honor Society rolled in. There came the fine, nice boy who sawed away at the fiddle in assembly, a wizard in the chemistry lab, alone. The one who had been devastated by infantile paralysis was driven up in the family car, swinging out on crutches, a moment of heavy steel braces flashing. Most girls came in pairs, dressed in loose jeans rolled to the knees, bulky sweaters tied over their shoulders. No tits swelled in the Honor Society. Smiles creased nearly all those freshly scrubbed faces—good, Christian, dues-paying faces. I thought I caught a glint of a green V-8 Ford cutting the corner right after Meredith walked up, long-leggedly, in a poplin raincoat. For suddenly, she too was there.

Her expression was big-eyed, concerned, more delighted to be on an Honor Society hayride than anywhere else on earth. I watched her as I would a classic movie I'd seen many times before. Nestled in the hay, our backs bouncing against the slats as we pulled out, I quoted some poetry to her. *A jug of wine, a loaf of bread—and thou beside me singing in the wilderness—Oh, wilderness were paradise enow!* A line that had seemingly sprung from memory like that (I had rehearsed its resonance for an hour that afternoon) must surely impress her. And how I ducked my head a little bashfully, peeling a strand of straw—she must surely be touched by the sensitivity there, the mark of one above the rough, ignorant manner of most Joes. Of Pancho. Her eyes were on me when I turned back, more brilliant than ever. "Look, Johnny . . ."

"Yes."

"Let's get everybody to sing 'Moonlight Bay.' " She put her thumb and middle finger in her mouth and whistled like a man. I'd forgotten she was president of the Honor Society, someone to take charge. "O.K., everybody, listen. We're going to sing 'Moonlight Bay.' Join in now. *We were sailing alonnnggg . . .*"

That song was followed by another, everyone smiling idiotically across the hay. I'd never liked community singing, feeling more a fool than usual, especially during movie shorts where a jumping ball told you what word you were on, but I wasn't about to let Meredith down. Then someone suddenly flew into a wild somersault, others following. That I didn't mind seeing, particularly when a girl's blue jeans became tight and showed her panty imprint. Meredith didn't perform a somersault—spontaneously breaking the rules not her style. She whistled again. "Please, everybody, we'd better stop somersaulting, somebody might fall off. They told us to sit back during the ride."

We ate an outdoor meal that evening in Scout Park, which was in a wooded area a few miles from town. Bare electric lights were strung by cords between trees, and fires leaped from the concrete-based grills. The wienies were cracked and burned on the outside, nearly frozen on the inside. We made them disappear in baths of French's mustard, and munched on them through cold buns. We were allowed Cokes, a decided privilege, some of us jiggling the bottles up and down with our thumbs over the top in order to send foam leaping up into the branches. For further fun, we roasted marshmallows on the ends of long sticks, burning our tongues when we finally tried to swallow them. I ate as much as possible, trying to prove to Meredith and the world I had a ravenous appetite, a mark of manliness.

And while I had my mouth full, the stout girl from physics class barged up babbling questions which I tried to comprehend. I worked my jaws, lips sealed on the chew, watching Meredith out of the corner of my eye. She was talking subduedly to the luminous-eyed boy who had been voted the class's Most Handsome, a model student who never got in any trouble. They didn't seem to be saying much to each other, just going through polite motions. There was a cast to Meredith's face I hadn't acknowledged before, a sort of vacant look

134

that would be disturbed by anything breaking the usual appearance of things. She shot a veiled glance my way that asked how dare I attract a girl beside me, even a fat one. I felt a novel surge of resentment toward her, and, last wad of wienie and soft bread down the esophagus, I had the new chilling urge to ease beside her and whisper something like, "Suck it, baby." That would free me from bondage for sure.

Instead, fires still flickering, I got her to lean against a tree with me, one foot propped up behind us. "What do you really think you want?" I asked. "You know. In life."

"I'd like to go to this girls' college down in South Carolina," she said. "My mother and grandmother went there. Oh, it's hard to think about after that. But I'd like to be able to cook and sew real good. Be able to make a good home."

Looking down at her scuffed, saddle-oxforded foot, her socks white and turned down neatly as always, I suddenly slipped into an old reverie of seeing us in a villa on the Riviera. She would be lying back in bed—decorously covered, of course—and I would be in silk pajamas and robe, out on a moon-washed balcony looking melancholy. Why I was so melancholy I didn't know; but she was sorry and wanted me to come to bed. Just a moment, dear, I called, I want to peck out a few thoughts on the typewriter first. And then, for no reason, the scene shifted to an ordinary apartment, a little on the grubby side. I was coming in the front door—unexpected, home early, dear—and there was some hazy individual arising from the top of Meredith on the couch. Looked a little like Pancho. Forgive me, she cried. The torture was exquisite, not so bad really. It was the truth suddenly revealed, and that was liberating. And the truth was you couldn't trust anyone, no matter how much you loved them. Finally, everyone was alone. "I, uh."

"Yes, what do you really want after you graduate?"

To machine-gun half the town? To burn down every one of those fine, large homes in the Pine Crest Addition? To buy a home there myself, the biggest of the lot naturally, and raise children who sported teeth braces and expensive, but sensible shoes? Maybe the best thing was just to get as far away from the town as possible, in every conceivable way. "I sort of would like to live in New York City."

"Johnny! With all those Yankees? Ugggg, how could you?"

Wide-eyed wonderment, aghast, as if I'd just announced I'd like to swallow nails. But were thoughts racing beneath those doe eyes, strange thoughts I'd never know about? She looked straight ahead as the truck tore back to town, letting us off one by one in front of our houses. Why did the older guy drive so fast—because he had no date himself and wanted to wrap things up in a hurry? At least, though, it gave me an excuse not to go through the trauma of a trembling lunge at her. The Honor Society wasn't big on smooching in public anyhow. "Oh, Johnny, it was so nice being with you on the hayride," she said, the truck backfiring in front of her home, hopping out.

"Don't take any wooden nickels," I called, debonair to the end.

Pancho carried an amused grin around for a couple of days after my evening outdoors with Meredith. The new un- written law that we wouldn't talk about her still held, but the strain finally proved too much. "What's the shit-eating grin for?" I said, at last.

"Boney, you're something. A hayride. With the Honor So- ciety. You're sure the make-out kid."

"I still don't see what's so goddamn funny, asshole."

"Nothing, don't get so touchy," and he looked me straight in the eye, the corners of his mouth held down to fight off a grin. "Tell me one thing now. Just one thing."

"Well, what?"

"How come you're so cute?"

I started to hit him, right in the cafeteria line, with the sharp aroma of greasy soup and hamburgers dizzying the air. But he danced back, as he used to do as a nine-year-old at the Maple Street Pool, holding his nose the same way and giggling so his jugular seemed ready to pop. This was worse than my ever catching him rising from Meredith on a couch, worse because it was a kind of betrayal I had never imagined. She had told him my dialogue. I watched him dance away, hooting. "Know what she says, Boney? She says you're not her type!"

I watched him trot for the stairs, the victor, off to sit beside her in study hall and tease her so she would pound his shoulder. Off to walk with her after school and nuzzle her ear. Off to rub her stomach when she had pains there. But suddenly there was a note of shrillness in his laughter, something I couldn't quite put my finger on, that made me pause. . . .

Five

It came to each in his own way that preparations had to be made for something to do after graduation, no bones about it. For after the twelfth grade—after all those years of meeting each fall, a little taller, a little less innocent—the reunions were over. If left to ourselves we'd probably keep showing up every year until senility, going out for football and basketball and finding someone new to have a crush on. Graybeards in beanies. But adults pushed us on, asking over and over what our "plans" were. Those who had a "plan" were certainly fortunate. I kicked around the idea for awhile of applying to the Sorbonne, not sure of anything connected with it except the possibility of getting some pussy in civilized surroundings. But when mentioning places like the Sorbonne to my parents, a light went on in the eyes only a second before dimming completely. I noticed that my father's gray suit was getting awfully old, stains on the sleeves and trousers. And how long had it been since he'd bought a new pair of shoes? The *Sorbonne?* Was I crazy? How could I expect to come by enough money for that? It would take more than we had to even go the hundred miles away to the state university. But the local college was always available like an extension of high school, safe and secure and ever undisturbing to the mind. The thought of going there put me to sleep, although something was going to have to be done after graduation. I coped with the problem in the only way I knew how. By doing nothing.

Pancho traveled to various campuses, on the trail of an athletic scholarship. All had been impressed by those spectacular feats in Friday night games, but the answer always came back from the cold, crisp logic of daylight: speed, fine; movement, fine; but too light for college ball. I met him at the train station one night when he came back from Knoxville, limping down the steps, his grin painful and his face red. General Neyland himself had checked over his naked body, looking for old scars and bones that hadn't knit properly. "He covered every goddamn inch of me. Even my teeth. As if I was a horse." He had twisted his ankle on a forty-yard wind sprint, and then just gave up, going to the dressing room, putting on his clothes, and leaving without a word.

That night at the train station I could tell his heart was not in getting an athletic scholarship—and when he wasn't totally committed, he only went through the motions. He was not going to get a scholarship anywhere. If they could have transported Meredith twirling in maroon panties, the band tooting, the stands screaming while Pancho tried out on those practice fields, then he probably would have been drafted by

142

the Chicago Bears. But, no, those fields were far from home with a completely different way of doing things.

And without an athletic scholarship it was unlikely that Pancho could get in any college. You had to pay tuition to get in even the most jerkwater one. And then one day I was going through the hair-combing ritual in the concrete-floored lavatory: water on the comb, a part sliced on the left side, back with a finger-wave pressed in the front. Pancho entered, peed, and while washing his hands said, "You son of a bitch."

"What's the matter now?"

"That hair. You got too much hair."

And I noticed, for the first time, that under a strong light I could see some of his scalp shining through at the front of his hairline. He went through a jerky, frowning session with the comb, pulling off the gobs of raven-black hair that had become caught in the teeth and shaking his head. He held one large gob under my nose, as if I somehow were responsible. "Just look at that!"

"Aw, hair comes off on combs all the time," I said. "Don't worry about it."

"Don't *worry?* It's going, sure as shit, it's going. How come you're not losing your hair, too, Boney?"

The only thing that cheered him up was believing that the Sheik was developing a bald spot at the back of his head. Pancho liked to sit behind him in class now, gazing at what he claimed was the incipient space. To all who were interested he would point out the region, describing how the hair now over it was deceptive and that any sudden movement would put the hairless stretch in view. The Sheik, usually in a trance these days in class, would explode all at once: "Pancho, I'm going to coldcock you in about three seconds if you don't leave the back of my head alone."

"Listen to him. He can't take it cause he's losing his hair."

The night of the R.O.T.C. ball arrived, and Pancho escorted Meredith to it. He was a second lieutenant with a lone silver button on each shoulder of his tunic while she was a major in the Sponsor Corps. Usually at R.O.T.C. functions she wore her blue uniform with gold leaf insignia. But since this was a dance, boys holding girls, she had on a long, swirling evening gown. Technically, she outranked him and should have been taken to the ball by the one boy of comparable rank, Major Fats Dyer. But Fats had his own girl, and so the rules were bent. As we came closer to graduation, more and more of the rules were being bent. Those of us not in the R.O.T.C. sat up in the stands of the gym, dressed in our finest, hoping we might be allowed down on the floor when the dancing got underway. There were so few chances to hold a nice girl that no possibility was ever overlooked.

But, before the fun, we had to witness crack drill teams stomping around, good conduct medals or somesuch being presented, and the colors being paraded on high. The colors were precisely why I wasn't an R.O.T.C. cadet now myself. Through two years I had buckled as well as I could under the R.O.T.C. regimen, even winning minor merit my first year as a squad leader. Our leaders were real-live army men, a sergeant and a major, both Southerners. Major Connerly walked around with his hands on his hips a lot, his uniform splattered with grease stains and his shoes carrying evidences of the barnyard. He was rather eccentric. In assembly some guest speaker would be babbling away—a reverend or politician putting us to sleep—when Major Connerly would suddenly rise and interrupt him. "What you're saying is a bunch of horse hockey," he told a startled and sissified college dean, who was extolling the virtues of peace to us. "Boys that follow that kind of doo doo will end up sucking hind tit. People never learn to lead till they've had the bejesus beat out of 'em." Our principal, whose eyes rolled when any profanity or reference to sex came up, never made a move against the Major no matter what the provocation. Like the rest of us, he was probably terrified of him. Rumor had it that the Major carried an army-issue forty-five at all times, inside his buttoned-up tunic, under his belt.

Sergeant Blackwell was the Major's opposite. A tall, fiercely good-looking man, with red cheeks and a mouth that had never smiled, his khakis were creased as sharply as a marine's, his shoes a mirror. He was a maniac for regulations and appearance, stopping you downtown on the street even if your cap was cocked a little too far to the side. His idea of humor was to stroll crisply past a line of cadets at inspection arms, then suddenly wheel backward and snatch a rifle from someone's hands so the boy fell over. He collected money from us for all the extras—the bullets we used in target practice, the manuals, the expenses of the annual ball. (He later went to the penitentiary for pocketing this money, having excluded himself from the stiff law-and-order strictures he preached. Sadly, our class had long graduated by the time his uniform changed from O.D.'s to stripes.) At the beginning of my senior year Sergeant Blackwell told me, in the mothball-reeking supply room, that I had been chosen to carry the colors.

Some honor. The other guys had been picked to lead companies and platoons, decked out in officers' finery, strutting around with pretty sponsors in blue by their side. The ignominy of being saddled with the flag. But then, of course, he laid it on thick about patriotism, respect for the emblem of Our Country, service above self—all the reasons given by those who send others into the slaughter while they loll back in graft and gravy. "Do I have any choice, sir?" We had to call him sir, even though he was only a sergeant.

"You have no choice."

I thought. The flag staff fit down in a leather pouch that rested right on your balls. Not only ignominy was involved, but danger. Hoisting the colors once or twice before, filling in for a sick or injured boy, I had felt the pouch tear (wartime material was cheap) and the sharp staff jab through into my wadded-up and defenseless privates. But head must be held high, looking straight ahead, marching to the count. *Hup, hip, hut, four!* And I was the skinniest boy in the field of seniors, at the mercy of every breeze. It didn't occur to me that perhaps I was selected *because* I was so light and unsteady, that I might treat the Sergeant to the sight of someone flying upward on a gale and down into the gutter while he stood strong and powerful to the side in creased O.D.'s. I did not know much about sadism at the time, didn't even know the word. All I knew was that for the first time in my life I was going to make a stand for principle. "I am not going to carry the flag, sir. Get someone else."

"A boy should not think twice about the privilege of carrying this country's flag. I order you to carry it."

"I won't. I quit R.O.T.C. altogether."

Dropping out did not hold any of the terrors I had imagined. A sea of robot bodies, decorated by the loveliest and nicest of senior girls, would be drilling and standing at attention in itchy wool and listening to the Major's sudden and bizarre announcements, the Sergeant's standard bad news, while a handful of us had the privilege of lying back on a hill and jabbing blades of grass between our teeth. We played basketball while they held inspection. And we got haircuts only when we needed them. The Sheik had been one of the earliest dropouts, throwing in the towel after having to wear the wool uniform to school one hot fall day. One of his main horrors in life was the fear of sweating so girls would notice. So now the brotherhood of dropouts collected in the stands at the annual ball, giving warmth to each other, waiting for the chance to pounce on the gym dance floor and belly-rub. Mixed in with us were older boys discharged early from the service, exotic college boys home for Easter vacation, and town fellows who just showed up every time as many as fifty people gathered no matter what.

We couldn't crash the first dance number of the evening; that was reserved, while the lights dimmed, for each cadet and his girl. Pancho took Meredith in his arms, holding her hand up rigidly, as if signaling a right turn, going mechanically through the motions. She leaned her head gently on his shoulder, seemingly weary. The tune was "Dream," as rendered by Fuzzy Powell and his Rhythm Makers, an off-key aggregate who let loose for the one or two school dances we had a year. Capt. Ernie Peoples, a beautiful smile on his lips, bent Sally Jane back, his bad knee socked in there, keeping his eyes open for buddies to nod to. On the last dance before intermission the first crashers hit the floor in a pincher movement. And while Sergeant Blackwell headed to cut off infiltration from the left, the battle-wise veterans among us cut unnoticed from the right into the mass of churning, clutching bodies. I felt my way along the wall, where I had cracked my head many times at basketball, and then, coast clear, side-stepped over to Pancho and tapped him on his stiff shoulder. "Cutting in," I said. The rules forbade any argument; once tapped, you had to let go.

"Oh, Johnny," Meredith said, arms out immediately, inviting me to come socking in. "I'm so glad you could make it." As if I'd been invited. I did my two standard steps to one side, then turned for a "dip." She felt too light to be true, her evening gown crinkly to the touch and giving off a powdery bouquet. Not wanting to repeat all I knew, the two-step and a dip, I began whipping around in a circle, causing the floor finally to spin. Stopping then to just stand there, rocking from side to side, I brought her soft hand up high against my heart. What if I wasn't her type? She was *my* type because I knew of no other girl to love. But I would never hold her any closer than at this dance I had just crashed. And now someone was tapping me. Oh, God, Sergeant Blackwell?

"Go take a breather, buddy. I'd like to dance with this girl."

It was Toby MacKarren, home from Sewanee U. His hair on top was trimmed a quarter-inch from the bone, his meaty cheeks glistened from a recent shaving, and he wore on his feet a pair of slightly soiled white bucks. I backed off, proud that he had tapped me and therefore approved of my taste. A college student from Sewanee! I had spied him in the Chocolate Bar that afternoon, lounging back in a booth with his arm comfortably on the back of the seat, saying, "Where can a man get a pint of liquor in this dump? Doesn't anybody drink around here?" Jesus, he was sophisticated. And now he was bringing Meredith's hand around to perch on the top of his butt, gliding her forward in a Sewanee, skater-type dance step. He seemed to be talking right into the top of her head at the same time. At the end of the number he threw her hand out, dislodging his hold, and walked away. Throughout intermission Pancho kept getting fruit punch for Meredith, following where she wanted to stand for the moment. She changed stations several times, I noticed.

On the first fast number after intermission Pancho fell into what looked like a half-waltz, half-hoedown. He would lead Meredith from side to side, right-turn signal up, and then suddenly break loose to stomp in and out like a drum major. Those times his cousin Mary Sue had tried to teach him how to cut a rug had evidently not paid off. Pancho, like me, just couldn't work up any enthusiasm for jitterbugging. It wasn't like football or pool, things that allowed you to concentrate. Here the girls were all the time shaking their butts in rhythm, puckering their lips and lifting eyebrows to the beat, and expecting a hand or foot to arrive at a certain spot on schedule. That was what got me, their *expecting* things. In slow, up-close dancing you could make up steps or even stop dancing technically altogether. Sometimes, a girl plastered against you, the nib of her pelvis striking home, you might daydream, eyes shut, that the two of you were grinding away in the buff. Who could do that with the eye-rolling jitterbug? But boys who *could* jitterbug well—like Jockey Joe Mahoney who wore bow ties and heavy, crepe-soled shoes—seemed to have a more casual, easy relationship with girls, understanding them perhaps. But no matter what, you could count on the authorities, with help from the Rhythm Makers, to call on enough fast ones a night to shatter all slow-dance fervor. I was immobilized during every furious rhythm.

And that was when I saw Toby MacKarren cut in on Pancho. It didn't seem too unusual then—a well-muscled boy in white bucks, striding over, tapping Pancho near his second lieutenant's silver button. Meredith looked up, as I remembered she had countless times at me: eyes wide, mouth open in wonderment and expectation. Pancho, his R.O.T.C. collar seeming too tight, backed away in a stiff, jerky nod. Nothing really out of the ordinary. But how that image sticks. If a later development of science could have recorded that moment on tape, I would have shown it over and over—in rehashing the game—as the play that changed the flow of action and led to its ultimate conclusion. The song was the "Jersey Bounce." Toby did a little skip, twirling Meredith out and bringing her back by the fingertips. They smiled at each other, a secret sort of smile. And Toby put in a quick flick of his fingers on the beat, something I hadn't seen around our parts before and which was surely a Sewanee U.-kind of action. It was the smoothest dance of the evening. And Sergeant Blackwell caught him as it ended. They had words on the floor and then the Sergeant was propelling him toward the door where I was trying to squeeze into myself and disappear.

"You know better'n bust in here, MacKarren," the Sergeant was saying. "What makes you think you can come to an R.O.T.C. ball? A civilian."

"Because I was invited by someone," Toby said. "That's why."

"Well, no one has the authority to invite you."

Toby himself invited some of the other crashers to pile in his red Mercury for a spin to Bristol to check out a night club there. Hearing the motor race in the school parking lot, the door held open, I turned the offer down. It was still too advanced a move for me.

The Sheik, though, was one of the first to climb aboard. I went back to the stands, watching Pancho lead Meredith through the wrap-up number of the evening, "Goodnight, Sweetheart." Nothing really seemed, to the eye, to have changed. He still held up his right-hand signal, and she leaned her head wearily and casually on his shoulder. Everything unchanged; for I went home alone, my mother coming down the stairs to unlock the door and let me in.

Only by bits and pieces did I get glimmers of what was hidden from view. One night Pancho dropped by, as he had hundreds of times before, sitting across from me on the concrete ledge in front of my house. Usually we joked, told stories about the Sheik or Miss Godsey. This night, he said, "The bastard, I could kill him."

"Who?"

"Aw—down home. Thaddeus." He called his father always by his first name, spitting it out. It sounded too naked, private, when he got on the subject and I turned my head. I wished Pancho could talk about pussy like the rest of us. "He gets everything out of my mother, no matter what she promises me. She said she'd never see him again, or give him any money, promised me faithfully. . . ."

One rule down at Uncle Buford's was that Pancho's father would never come within a mile of it. Pancho's mother— Uncle Buford's sister—came and went, a mysterious woman who was treated by Pancho more like a child than a parent. In fact, he acted at times as if he were her guardian, watching her grow up and make mistakes. Home was so private, as secret to the rest of the world as your naked body, and guarded in the same way. There were the smells of home, the dishes for meals, the stories—the very little things that gave the place the rich feeling that always stayed in a part of your mind, the way smoke from your father's Chesterfields curled in the Sunday sunlight and the sound of meat frying from the kitchen. You might envy someone who lived in a fine brick home on a hill, someone whose father wheeled and dealed, but in the end you were left, and felt at ease only, with where you came from. My folks were dependable; if nothing else on earth, they were dependable. Put my father in a Houdini-type trunk and sink him to the bottom of the ocean, he'd still pop out in time to grab his lunch box and make it to the depot for his trick. He'd never missed a day's work in forty years, not one. And he had a full head of hair. Pancho's father was bald.

Meredith missed a few days of school, and came back to say that she had been on a visit to the South Carolina college her mother and grandmother had attended. Oh, she hoped they would accept her, admit her. As if there might be some doubt. It was a strict, all-women's school, just the place you'd pick for the nicest girl in our class. They didn't even allow boys to hold girls' hands on campus, the story went. Pancho wore his itchy wool uniform to school on R.O.T.C. drill days that spring, his second lieutenant badge looking a little sad now among the boys displaying proud captain and major ranks, sissy boys who couldn't play football or run a rack of pool but gloried in spit and shine. This wasn't like Pancho, fitting into a secondary role and not even ridiculing the R.O.T.C. in private. It must have been Meredith's influence in some way, I figured, for hadn't it always been Pancho's idea to drop out altogether if you couldn't make the first rank at something, better by far to stand along the sidelines than to be slotted in a halfway role?

And then came the moment I watched Pancho tease Meredith as he had done a hundred times before. It was beside her locker where she was squatting down to get books for her next class. He suddenly snatched the thick literature text (from Chaucer to Percy Bysshe Shelley, where English stopped for us) and held it aloft. She made the usual grab for it, eyes wide and mouth gaping as if it were the first time he'd pulled the stunt. She jumped for it. No good, he just lifted it higher. Then I saw a cloud pass her face, barely noticeable. She squatted again to get the rest of her books.

"Want it?" Pancho teased, waving the text under her nose. She didn't look up. "Come on. Beg for it, and I might let you have it."

"Cut it out," she said, voice startlingly level. "I haven't got time to play silly games with you today. . . ."

And before my house, on the concrete ledge, he said, "Women," in an adultlike tone, "you can't count on a one of them."

His black mood hit him during classes, while he lined up a pool shot, and on our walks home from school. He would frown suddenly, dark eyes blazing, and look off to the side. It was hard being alone with him then, and only because buddies weren't required to talk was it bearable. What could you say? And then on one of our walks to the poolroom, he brightened; for no reason I could find, he seemed much happier, talkative. It was as if something in a removed, secret part of his mind had clicked, a solution found. He chortled over the latest thing in the Sheik's life, how an old, hard-of-hearing woman had thought his name was Garbage instead of Ghazi. He related how Jitterbug Watson had thrown an epileptic fit recently on his front porch when someone had tried to borrow showfare from him. Delving into other people's miseries in the way he liked, his old self again.

And so late one night he tooted the horn of the V-8 out front. Probably wants to make a run by Meredith's, I thought. And, sure enough, that was where he was heading, shifting into second, pulling on his nose pleasurably before bringing the stick down into third. But this ride turned out differently from the others—for a few blocks down the road, he reached over, opened the glove compartment, and brought out a pint of Four Roses. "Get a load of this," he said. He brought it up quickly, let a gurgle go down, and then shook his head like a grownup. His jugular stood out the way it did when he inhaled deeply.

"I thought you said you'd never take a drink."

"I know," with the same swift glance, and chortle, he gave when admitting he'd played dirty. "I lied. Take one yourself."

I did, holding my tongue over the bottle and letting only a trickle wet my mouth. Then I shook my head mightily, too. That's what I liked most about drinking, the head shaking and the bottle passing. And you couldn't get hooked on raw whiskey by a drink or two, either, whereas bringing cigarette smoke in your lungs sentenced you to life there. And now, after four or five trickles of Four Roses, I could scream, "YAAAA, hoooo! Fuckey, fuckey!" Right out the open window, as we sailed past the Reverend Lovelace's house. Cutting into the Pine Crest Addition, Pancho had a strange, secret grin going, driving faster than usual and with more assurance. At the brick-and-stucco home he stopped, motor racing. All lights out in the house, it seemed more removed from my life than ever—sealed off, barricaded, Buckingham Palace. "Yaaaa, hoooo! MEREDITH, I love you! But my buddy took you away from me! My buddy, PANCHO!"

Before he took off in a screech of tires, he raised another one of those long, gurgling drinks. Back before my house, taking on the same look he had when he thought he spotted a bald spot on the Sheik, he said, "Boney, you're a born rummy if I've ever seen one. You just can't leave it alone, now can you?"

Letting myself in with the skeleton key that any burglar could duplicate at the five-and-ten, I held my breath the best I could, through the dark living room, up the stairs, and into my room—exhaling with an, "It's me, Momma," when challenged, enunciating the words. Safely in bed, having gotten away with a spree, I breathed in and out in great excitement. Pancho's drinking now. Boy oh boy, nothing's going to be the same again. And there wasn't anything that pleased the mind then so much as change. No matter what it was.

My first reaction on hearing about the injury was one of excitement, too. Change, something happening, news to follow. And then a quick rush of guilt made me ashamed that I would welcome such events. My mother was telling me about it on Saturday morning, and my sleep-drugged brain had trouble sorting out the facts. At first I thought the Sheik was involved. Surely he was the logical one to receive any trouble the Lord might deal out to his family. "Poor Mr. Mansur," she said, "now to have this happen . . . the hospital . . . it looks so very bad . . . so sudden. . . ."

"Ghazi's cracked up the car, I know it."

"No, it's Leila. She fell from a horse."

Leila? She'd never harmed anyone in her life. She stood long hours by the cash register down at the Roxy, the one member of the family her father could trust. She followed the rules to the letter, making good grades at school, being quiet in class. She wore black skirts and starched white blouses a lot, a faint shadow of hair showing on her upper lip in certain light. You tended to overlook her, like a fireplug you were accustomed to passing every day. In early evening as I would stroll by the Roxy, homeward bound and groggy from the poolroom, I would glimpse her leaning back behind the register against a cabinet. We waved whenever our eyes met, a shy smile jumping from her dark face. Our common bond was the Sheik—or *Ghazi* as she insisted he be called—and in every conversation she somehow got his name brought up, enumerating feats of prowess that I had trouble connecting with the fellow I knew. He, on the other hand, barely tolerated her existence as a person—ordering her to bring him milk, telling her to get out of the living room when he brought the gang in, on occasion getting her to shine his shoes.

It had happened shortly after dawn, of a cloudless, dewy day. She had gone for the weekend—one of her few holidays —to the Presbyterian camp in the mountains toward Asheville. It was called a "religious retreat," something my crowd avoided like the plague because of the innumerable prayers and Spartan atmosphere. She had been on a trail ride, the last in line, mounted on a frisky colt that hadn't been used often on that particular path. But Leila hadn't complained when the horse was given her; it wouldn't have been her style. She wanted to be more southern than the southerners, more American than apple pie. Didn't all mountain girls know how to handle horses by second nature, being swung on bareback by their daddies by the time they could walk? The colt had shied at a turn, reared up, and Leila had slid off—not screaming, protesting in any way. The horse had kicked her in the head.

Now she lay in a private, second-floor room of the hospital. What could I say to the Sheik, his father, when it came time for some words? I cut down the corridor, looking for the room number, afraid. Those antiseptic smells that leaped out at you, the quick views from partially opened doors of old gray men, inverted bottles above their beds, needles in their arms. Everyone hushed, awed by trouble. The Sheik became jumpy even if the word *hospital* came up. What would he be like now that he must keep vigil in one? I found him outside the door, smoking. His eyes had a bright intensity, as if he might be pleased to have been torn out of deep lethargy and a standard way of looking at things. "Boney, what do you think?"

"Aw, she'll be all right, Ghazi. I know she will be."

"Of course!" He laughed, those eyes now too bright, clutching my forearm. "Boney, I want to ask you one thing. Now you tell me the truth, you skinny bastard."

"O.K."

"Haven't you been knocked goofy in football? Haven't you had a blow on your head about every week of your life?"

"Sure, all the time. Remember when I caught the baseball between the eyes? You guys had to carry me home. I didn't know where I was for two days. My momma had to feed me by hand."

"That's right, that's right!" His words came in machine-gun fashion, almost too quick for his mouth. He grabbed my school jacket that had faded to an almost colorless state. "I don't remember a thing about the second half of the Kingstown game last fall, either. Sure, sure. Then everything cleared. That happens in nature. And, Boney, they're flying a specialist in from Nashville. Everybody says he's the best in the country, and he's from Nashville. How can you beat somebody who's the top of a profession wanting to live in Nashville? Now that doc's all right, ain't he? You know damn well he is. Hey, you want to have a look? She doesn't look much different from always."

Inside, layers of tobacco smoke hung suspended in the air, and a phalanx of strange men—Lebanese uncles and cousins —sat comfortably around the lone bed, drawing on cigars and pipes and cigarettes. Now, suddenly thrown in close proximity to their mystifying world, I wanted nothing more than to be one of them—a Lebanese myself. And when they started speaking their quick, hand-waving language, I nodded and smiled as if I understood. Leila did look about the same as usual: her features unmarked, pale, with a slight bead of sweat on her upper, shadowed lip. There was a white bandage, with tape, around the top of her head, and that was the only sign that she had been hurt—that and the fact that her eyes were closed. She seemed to be having but a fitful sleep, lying on one side a moment and then turning fiercely over on the other. When she made a turn, trying to move her lips it seemed, the Sheik spoke. "Why, she's going to be talking pretty soon. Anybody moving around like that has got to be O.K. Isn't that right, Boney?"

They operated an hour after the Nashville specialist came in, and then the call went out that blood was needed. Pancho was ahead of me in line, his veins swelling as big as sticks when the arm clamp was tied on. His dark red blood jumped into the waiting bottle, taking hardly more time than a cough to fill, and then he made jokes. He had been terribly quiet beforehand. As I pushed back my sleeve, a tired-eyed doctor with a stethoscope hanging against his white smock said, "Son, you don't have to give any if you don't want to. I think we'll have enough."

"But I'm O.K., doc. I'm on the tennis team."

He told the nurse to take only a half pint, causing me to blush. And then Pancho said, "If you have any left over at the end, you can always give Boney a pint." It got a laugh.

But blood came out of me, I was relieved to see; I became a donor. Then Mr. Mansur invited the whole team down to the Roxy to have anything we wanted, all we could eat. As we jostled each other down the corridor, sleeves kept rolled up to display our badges of blood-donor's tape, alive, I spotted Margaret Moody yanking away on an X-ray machine, breasts raised. I didn't know whether under the circumstances to get excited or not, being now in a hospital as a good Samaritan and not recruiting for the back seat of a car. It was another world impinging on my present one, a different set of circumstances, and I had trouble turning my neck to say hello. She didn't call out to me, either, going on about her business. How could a girl who took balls and all have a job like a regular person, anyhow, saying hello and good-bye just like anybody? But down at the Roxy, putting away a bowl of Mexican chili, swigging a Nehi, nodding assent to a second helping, I kept remembering how full her breasts looked and how her white-stockinged calves swelled. It was strange, but grieving just seemed to lead to hunger and thoughts of sex.

Mr. Mansur was not quite as cheerful as the Sheik. He shook all our hands, made sure we'd all eaten to the breaking point, and gave the Sheik commands in a rough, good-natured manner that pleased us all—but there was a dim light in his eye when you caught his expression unawares, a light from the past none of us could comprehend. You caught this dim light in many grownups' eyes from time to time. Mr. Mansur did

158

not look—certainly did not talk and act—like any other father. He was dark, with large, generous features, and a delivery of lightninglike broken English that you had to learn to understand, like pidgin Latin. The Sheik grew upset with his father on the least pretense, going into rages. "Why can't he *speak* like everybody else! This *whatta you wanna eatta today* stuff is driving me crazy, *killing* me! How can I invite anybody home?"

But Mr. Mansur did his duty, you sensed, just like my father did, and he would never do a bad deed against anyone. Not many grownups fell into that category—certainly not a lot of representatives of the church, Boy Scout Movement, and the school system. Looking at Mr. Mansur, the way he stood behind the register where Leila usually was, I wished I could give him a half a pint. We all left the Roxy for the Buffalo—just like always—banging each other's blood-donor arm, whooping it up, repeating the nice kidding we would give Leila when she woke up. The Sheik led the way, bellowing.

She died the next day. My mother woke me up early to tell me. I looked for the Sheik down hospital corridors, in the waiting room, at his house, the Roxy, everywhere. I hung around the Buffalo, all of us trying to admit the truth. She was such a fixture, with us from earliest memories. And now, cut off. She wouldn't go to college, marry, have children, nothing. Forever she would be behind that register, being good, faithful. She wouldn't even have time to be mean. How could you acknowledge such a fact? Having given up finding the Sheik, I just ran into him a block from home. He seemed to be just standing there, right in the middle of the sidewalk, not moving.

"John."

"It's so . . ."

"If . . ."

"What?"

"If . . . I could have just had five minutes with her awake . . . just one minute . . . just for her to have come awake and look at me and let me say I liked having her around. . . . That's all."

"What?"

"It's not fair. It's so goddamn unfair!"

Leila had been added to the growing list of those who hadn't made it through. Bunch Ledford, a smiling, apple-cheeked boy of a few years back had been bitten on the leg by a dog as he cheerfully delivered the afternoon paper. Since graduation exercises from high school were just around the corner, he hadn't reported the bite immediately, so the story went, for fear he wouldn't be allowed to take part. Being a good boy, not wanting to cause a fuss. The dog had been mad, and Bunch had died screaming in the hospital. Of all scare stories in town, that one took the cake—topping all iron-lung accounts of infantile paralysis and deaths by drowning. Anyone who could recount stories of being near his isolated room and hearing the screams was listened to with all ears, mouths gaping. Nothing could save poor Bunch, nothing at all. Strapped down like Frankenstein's monster, he was under the breeze from a roomful of fans hitting him from all directions. The call had gone out for the donation of fans—like that for blood—and a next-door neighbor had lent the hospital three. After Bunch's funeral, those fans went wrapped up to the attic, never to be used again, shamed objects. For some time after the death, I would check in with my mother every time a dog came within a block, wondering if I shouldn't be rushed to the hospital. And through the night, dog or no dog, I crept to the refrigerator for a swig of bottled ice water, knowing that if you could take water you didn't have hydrophobia.

And there were the slow, drawn-out deaths, each step proclaimed along the way—someone with a bad rheumatic heart, someone wasting away with a mysterious blood disease. Buddy Bradshaw had been like everyone else, swimming in the Maple Street Pool, hooting in the drive-in over milk shakes with some girl. And then suddenly he was out of it, a pale ghostly figure seen driving around late at night by himself or down very early on Sunday morning to buy a magazine at the newsstand. Ashamed. He had leukemia, and he lasted one year after high school. Frederick Jackson had never even made it to high school, going under in a pond the summer after getting out of junior high. Built strong as a bull and having a beard before any of us, he had simply gone under on a Boy Scout trip—with no cry of help, no splashing. They found out later he just couldn't swim. We all passed by his coffin at the funeral home, candles flickering to the side, a waxwork figure of old Frederick stretched out on silk, one hundred percent out of it now. I remembered that he had had one of the biggest ones on display in the shower after phys. ed., and wondered who else might carry such memories of him through life. The adults seemed terribly touched by us trooping by, dressed in our Sunday best, respectful and scared out of our wits. I was one of the pallbearers at the final services, struggling with my end of the coffin down the long concrete steps to the sleek, purring hearse. Ernie Peoples was mad that he hadn't been selected as a pallbearer. I told him it was no picnic, but was secretly glad I had won out ahead of him.

At Leila's funeral her coffin rested in a snowbank of flowers, a too-sweet scent reaching all the way to the back row where I sat with Pancho. Mr. Mansur had picked boys and men who had been at the religious retreat with Leila for pall-bearers, one—his pale face seeming ready to crack—the man who had chosen the horse for Leila and helped her into the saddle. There were more songs than words at the funeral, and then we all ambled out into a beautiful sunny day. It wasn't long until some of us were down at the Buffalo, others making dates on the phone, going to movies or eating steaming food our mothers dished up. Everyone returned to his normal life, everyone but the Sheik.

Again no one could find him. After the funeral he disappeared—his father's car missing also—all of us sure he would be heard from from the bottom of some ravine. He did demolish the car three days later in Asheville, and his father had to send him busfare to get home. He didn't say where he'd been all that time, what he had been up to. He was extraordinarily quiet from the way he had been in the past, shooting pool in an offhand, lackadaisical way and not seeming to care who won or lost. He smiled occasionally, but only if it were a terrific joke, nothing average or stale. He seemed to be sleep-walking or in the grip of some profound insight that barred his dealing ever again intimately with us. Knowing the old Sheik well, though, a few of us thought his present mood was just a lull before a storm. He would one day go berserk and do something outrageous to make up for lost time—like blowing up the high school—and then he would return to normal. None of us was prepared for what he did do.

The Sheik got married. The one who had had constant trouble with girls, the one who couldn't be trusted to earn a dollar on his own—he got married. Dropped out and got a job. The bride was one of those innumerable nice girls, someone you'd seen around since it all began. If you didn't have a crush on this type of girl, you took for granted she'd be working out geography questions into eternity, monumentally vomiting into her text after a cafeteria lunch (or, worse, catching you), and being always out for girls' basketball. Now that the Sheik was married—ran off secretly to Virginia to do it, like pulling a burglary—I remembered seeing him with her fleetingly in a drugstore, walking down the school hall, and once on a street corner arguing. I had taken for granted that nothing other than what met the eye was going on. *Marriage?* That was a strange world that happened to people only at the end of movies—or was in effect at the beginning, like Judge and Mrs. Hardy. You just couldn't imagine Andy marrying Polly Benedict. It would all be over then, *finis*. Something on the order of dying. For marriage was joining those who controlled you, being grown up. Its people were all over on the other side of a great chasm, people whose innards had been exchanged in the middle of the night by some swift force from outer space, but who still tried to pass as ordinary human beings. The bride's name was Evelyn. She and the Sheik set up housekeeping on the ground floor of his father's house, Mr. Mansur relegated to upper, out-of-sight regions.

The gang came to call as soon as decently possible. The Sheik sat in the best chair, a large, overstuffed one, wearing, his legs crossed, a pair of leather slippers. It was early evening, a time usually spent running off a rack or two at the Buffalo. Pancho, sitting nervously on the edge of a straight chair, pulling his nose, said, "How's the married life, Sheik?" You always said that, like offering condolences.

"How the hell should I know?" he said. "I just got into it."

"I heard that," Evelyn said, swinging in from the kitchen. She seemed nicer looking now, blonde hair combed back neatly, her body looking stocky and firm. She wore an apron, but I could still see her vividly in a gym suit. "Ghazi, we're out of milk. We won't have any for breakfast tomorrow."

"I'll go out and get some."

"It's either that or do without cereal."

"I said I'd go out. Lord!"

Such a fuss over a simple thing. At my house milk just mysteriously appeared, my mother pouring. The Sheik put on his shoes, grabbed a bill from Evelyn's purse, and led the way out of his house. He suggested on the sidewalk that we check in the Buffalo for a moment before he got the milk and returned home. "See who's there," he said. Out of the milk money he bought a beer—the appropriate drink of a married man, we felt—and then he took on Pancho in a game of straight. He lost, as always, some things never changing; lost all the rest of the milk money. "Well, we'll just have to do without cereal in the morning," he said. "Who the hell needs it anyhow? I'm no errand boy, I know that." He stuck around for another half hour, yawning and complaining that the poolroom haze was burning his eyes. It didn't seem any stronger than usual. He bounced a ball from an idle table back and forth on a side cushion, saying finally, "Aw, I'm tired of this place." He walked out alone; for home.

The Sheik now had to arise at five thirty in the morning for the drive to the trucking company in a nearby town. He held one of those strange, unlikely jobs that only married men seemed to find, a day confined to a sunless office and dealing with reams of paper. He was a dispatcher or accountant or glorified office boy, something or other; he had trouble, in his present groggy and married mind, explaining actually what he did do. He hadn't considered working at the Roxy, the most logical spot for him, claiming he would get in a fight with his father after five minutes on the job; we all felt, though, the real reason was that he just couldn't bear standing behind the register where Leila had stood so long. He would never listen willingly to any of the music that had been played at her funeral.

He drove over to the neighboring town in a car pool composed of married men or bachelors too old for school or handouts from home any longer. On Saturday afternoon he sometimes showed up at the Buffalo with a few of them. They all had pot guts, odd but nonflashy clothes, and genial, nonpushy ways. You could beat them easily at pool, because they had difficulty concentrating and taking the game seriously. They liked to tell tall tales about the drives to and from work, apparently the only time they made real decisions and were on their own. A divorcee occasionally rode with them on the early-morning run, the secretary to the owner of the trucking firm. In the back seat, in the gloom before sunrise, she would let a chosen one or two come awake by playing with her large breasts. There were lots of stories about her. And they told of a co-worker, a devoted member of the Church of the Brethren, who didn't allow swearing or stories of sex and drinking when he drove his car. The Sheik had drawn wangs and balls and gaping, hairy receptacles all over the frosted back windows in answer—telling how the saintly driver, eyes on the road, had kept chirping about the virtues of the good and clean life while startled pedestrians on the neighboring town's streets had backed off at the sight of the passing artwork. "Ain't that Ghazi something," one said happily. "I don't think I could stand that job without him."

One good thing about the Sheik's marriage was that you always knew where to find him now. Unless he was at the Buffalo or the Roxy, you could count on him being at home. Many times he would be playing an early-evening game of poker with his car-pool cronies on the dining room table or drinking beer and chortling with them around the sealed-up fireplace. Nearly always some male visitor would be there, others coming and going like clockwork. If you had a problem, if you just needed a laugh, you headed to the Sheik's—Evelyn given no more than a hello-and-good-bye nod and a thanks for bringing you a fresh can of beer. The Sheik liked his easy chair by the shaded lamp, slipper shod, eyes growing increasingly bloodshot as eleven o'clock approached. But even if he nodded off, you still didn't have to leave until you felt like it, never worrying about locking the front door. Others might be trooping in after you—for a place to drink after-hour beer or sleep off the night on the couch.

One night Evelyn, whom we'd all forgotten about, even seemingly the Sheik, had on a new dress. It had no belt, wasn't drawn in at the waist at all, and pooched out a little in the front. "Married life is making you fat," Pancho said.

"It's not fat," she said. We all turned to the Sheik, who held a sheepish grin.

Evelyn sat more and more with the gang in the evening, her feet in sensible shoes hiked up on the coffee table, palms resting on her swollen belly. You tried to keep from looking there, but couldn't help it. Now and then, quite unexpectedly, she would break into some bizarre thought we never knew she held—like what if there was life on Mars or wonder if ants have a sense of pain. No one listened, though, cutting her off whenever she paused for breath. For she brought a strange element into our midst, tending to cool down our hottest anecdotes and put a damper on the kidding. We looked to the Sheik for help, but he was generally lost in his new-found grin and said the least to Evelyn of anyone. His words came, when at all, in pique: "Who ate all the peanut butter?" "Where's my handkerchief?" "You took my matches!"

The Sheik and Pancho kept up their running set of insults

and arguments, nothing changed there since childhood. It would be getting about time to close up shop for the night at the Sheik's when Pancho would say, hooding his eyes with his hand, "Look at the fat boy. He hasn't walked two steps tonight. Pretty soon he's going to want us to carry him around on that easy chair like he was Mahatma Gandhi."

"Mahatma *Ghazi,* you mean," Evelyn said.

"That's it," Pancho said, hooting, pulling his nose, his jugular pushing out.

"All right, Pancho," the Sheik said, flying from his chair, fists drawn. "You keep talking with that vein jumping out on the side of your neck like that and I'm going to belt you one in the goddamn teeth. I can't stand looking at that vein!"

They stood facing each other, snorting, feet pawing the ground, just the way it used to end up in the vacant lot, although this time the Sheik was in bedroom slippers. There was a frozen moment, a return to childhood before all the risks they were taking passed through their heads. Slowly the wind went out of their argument, whatever had triggered it.

A mellowness settled in then, some of us fondly remembering the fights and escapades of yesterday. It was reassuring in a way, proof that we hadn't moved entirely into a new ball game, no matter how many marriages and graduations there might be. If this had been a normal household, everyone an adult, the Sheik probably would have tossed his guest out. But, no, he suddenly switched moods—in keeping with his old style—and became even hostlike. "Look, Pancho. Sleep on the couch tonight if you don't want to go home to Uncle Buford's. You know where the sheets and blankets are. You can fix Evelyn and yourself breakfast tomorrow after I'm gone. But, God almighty, man, don't start hooting at me with that vein jumping anymore."

Pancho nodded, the nearest he could ever come to saying he was sorry. They had patched up differences once more and were old friends again.

But no one could say where new problems might arise, everything moving so quickly and freshly these days. Evelyn's mother started coming over more often, now that the pregnancy was coming down the homestretch, giving Pancho a run for his money on lengths of visits. You might think a momma in such circumstances would be bringing bassinets or something, feeding Evelyn iron and making sure she got her rest. Not her. She was younger than most mommas, hair dark and bobbed, a plump and bosomy body. The Sheik—not having had a real momma of his own—was at first tremendously happy to have her around, calling her, "Momma Wilson," and expecting apple pie and roast turkeys to come flying out of the oven immediately. Even long after his illusions and hopes had been shattered, he still clung to "Momma Wilson" as his term of address.

My first meeting with her was when she sailed in the front door, faced the startled gang, and bellowed, "Lord, my dogs is killing me. Somebody crack me a cold one."

She sat with her small stockinged feet up on the coffee table, drinking beer straight from the can, every so often tugging on her girdle. What could you say to such a momma? We tried the weather, church news, and a commentary on *Gone with the Wind*. She chattered brightly, no matter what the topic, turning suddenly to her daughter: "You should have been down at the Princess Shop today. They had a sale on just your size."

"Momma, I'm big as a ship now. I can't wear my normal size. You should know that."

"Listen, Evelyn, to what I tell you. *Buy out of season*. You save money. How many times have I told you that?"

We certainly weren't going to sit around and bullshit about dress sales. What was going on here? We stood, drained the last juice from our cans, and said we had to shove off. The Sheik leaned forward, cracking his knuckles. "Where you boys going, the poolroom? Maybe I'll be down a little later."

"Who's that?" Momma Wilson said, pointing to me. I told her, and she asked about my own momma. "She's a fine lady." Everyone said that, I expected it. "And *that?*" toward Pancho. She raised her can for a long pull, lowering it slowly and with a faint smile. "I sure know your mom—*and* your daddy."

Pancho frowned on the way to the poolroom, as if Momma Wilson was the type of person who got on his nerves. But soon, in their crisscrossing at the Sheik's, a strange relationship developed between them. They sat up together on the couch, drinking Four Roses or beer, feet up, long after Evelyn and the Sheik had called it a night. They shared private jokes and kept a mock-serious battle running between them. On Sundays when the household ran dry—no matter how much had been stored away on Saturday—Pancho would announce, "O.K., I'll go to the bootlegger's if everybody will toss in a buck. I'll take your car, Big Momma."

That was what he called her now, Big Momma, and she seemed to enjoy it. Snarled from the side of his mouth, it denoted someone earthy, giving, and—sexy. "I'm not going to let you go off in my car by yourself, Pancho," she said. "You'd just go joy-riding all over town. Probably end up at that little Meredith Lancaster's house if I know you. Somebody go with him and make sure he comes right back."

"You come ahead with me then, Big Momma."

"No," the Sheik said. "She can just stay here. Why do you

have to be wet-nursed all the time, Pancho. Looks like a grown boy could go to the bootlegger's by himself."

Despite all mounting evidence before him, the Sheik still hoped that a mother would blossom who would stay indoors, give *him* a key, and make him promise to be a good boy and return home early. He yet dreamed of a mother who might crochet for hours by the light of the window.

"Aw, let her go with Pancho," Evelyn said. "That's what she wants to do."

They would come back from the bootleg run, cigarettes dangling from their lips, swigging beer wrapped in a brown paper bag, secret smiles plastered on. "Who's ready?" Momma Wilson would bellow, dealing out the cans. She would sigh heavily, chore done, and then take a seat in the middle of the couch, Pancho to one side, Evelyn to the other—all feet up. I wandered around, too jumpy and sex-wrought to sit long, wondering if I shouldn't call home to give my latest whereabouts of the day. Now that graduation was looming I had more freedom, but still had to check in with locations along the way as if I were an FBI agent. It was a little embarrassing. The Sheik sank deep into his easy chair, grin on, rising only for a fresh can, an inspired Dagwood, or the john. A gang trooped in and out, each new visitor going through his routine of jokes and hard-luck stories we all knew by heart. It was a scene you could imagine going on forever.

Six

And so that Saturday began as any number of them had. Pancho came by my house shortly after breakfast, dressed in an old gray sweater, holes in the sleeves, that he used only for weekends. We walked down to the Buffalo, not even having to say where we were headed, unthinkable that a Saturday would start off anywhere else. We breezed past the hot dog and beer counter at the front, its spicy aroma clearing our heads immediately for action. Balls clicked up and down the long, wide hall—men and boys in overalls, sweaters, a few in suits, leaning over green tables already, everyone equal and clean now at the beginning.

Pancho won a dollar from me, and then took on a country boy he had always had trouble with before. The balls rolled just right for Pancho this time, and—hard to believe —by the time we were hungry for hot dogs he had cleaned the country boy out and was over twenty-five dollars ahead. Twenty-five! I would have quit right then. But not Pancho. In mid-afternoon—as I was about to slip off to catch the Range Busters at the Sevier—Pancho got involved with old Curly in a game of straight. Surely only someone with a death wish at gambling, like the Sheik, would take on Curly, the second-best stick in the house. Curly would of course spot Pancho a certain number of points at the beginning—like a golf handicap—but no matter how much it was, you could count on Curly taking charge somewhere along the way and running rack after rack till your heart broke. He was that good.

No one knew exactly what Curly did on the outside, but in the poolroom he was an aristocrat. One time Humphrey had eased up to him and said, "Getting any poon tang, Big Shot?" and Curly had sniffed the air in total, prim disdain. He carried his own private stick in a leather case with metal snaps—something that could have held a clarinet—and he didn't drink beer, tell jokes, or get very friendly with anyone. He chalked his cue and aimed quickly, without a word, seemingly impatient to show his superiority and to get the dirty work over with in a hurry. Once I was up at daybreak for some reason, walking downtown, and passed old Curly carrying a lunch box. He didn't even nod, eyes averted, caught red-handed with an emblem of the employed. Did he stoke coal through the night somewhere, sit up as a male nurse, stalk through a downtown store as a night watchman? All I knew was that I felt sort of sorry for him then. He must be married.

Curly won the first game. He shot even quicker than

usual, a flick of the eye down table before clicking the ball into the slot, perhaps angry that Pancho—who should know his reputation, who had only been a little boy struggling to learn a couple of years ago—should now dare to challenge him. He won the second game, and then Pancho said, "Spot me ten more points, Curly. Come on."

"Why should I?" He was snapping the cue ball out and back against the rail in a tricky way with his fingers. He seemed bored.

"Because I'd give you a better game that way."

"O.K., I got no one else to shoot right now. Make it five."

Pancho won. Frowning, taking a long time to aim, listening stoically to Curly's complaints, he held on when his turn came to shoot, and won; the last three balls were sunk from very severe angles. Curly repowdered his right hand—he was a southpaw—ran sandpaper around the edge of his cue tip, and asked for a new cue ball. Now he was *really* going to get serious, no fooling around at all. And Pancho won again, more decisively than before. They were tied in games, even-steven in money. "All right, I'm taking those five points back I spotted you," Curly said.

"No." That was all Pancho said. No reason, no excuse, just one word: "No." It was as if he was too young to have to go into a meaningful reason. He just clung to the word like a dog to a bone. "No."

And it must have been infuriating to Curly who was used to calling the shots. I knew myself how infuriating Pancho could be at times, making you pound your head with your fists and roll on the grass, but this was the first time I saw this trait transferred into the grown-up world. Curly unscrewed his cue, placed the pieces in his snappy leather case, and started out. Pancho didn't budge, holding his cue with both hands, chin immobile on his arm. Curly got as far as the front door before he wheeled and came back. "All right," he said. "Let's play one more."

He came within a point of winning several times—a fraction of an inch in how a ball rolled making the difference—but he just couldn't take Pancho. It must have been maddening for him, coming so close, knowing Pancho had sprung out of nowhere, just a modicum of luck his way and then he'd be able to wipe the upstart out for good. But before he could go on, he must have more money; Pancho was not giving credit. It was early evening, around suppertime, when Curly said, "I'm going home to get some dough from my wife. Don't leave. I'll be right back."

A small crowd had now gathered around the table, and no one left his place as Curly raced out the door with his case. Pancho stalked around, chalking his cue one moment, sending me over to the counter for a Nehi the next. I would have been in seventh heaven to be in his shoes then, people's eyes on me, wallowing in the frills of success. Not Pancho. He kept glancing at the big Western Union wall clock. He needed to go on in that all-or-nothing way he had. The right to strut around with people watching was just wasted on him. And it came to all of us—Pancho first of all—that Curly might be having difficulties at home. Definitely I would have quit right then and there—walked out calmly, knowing I'd given him plenty of time to get back, then counting the money won over and over again in the secrecy of my locked room. My philosophy of life was that I could count myself a winner just by breaking even since losing was my standard fate. Why demand everything every time a little something came your way?

But Pancho tarried, holding the table, committed to all or nothing, until of course someone said, "Get old Dulaney. He'll take you on, Pancho."

Dulaney was the Number One Stick in town. Every time a particular kind of stranger would pop up in the Buffalo, decked out in straw hat and bib overalls, shooting like a woman at first but then showing a remarkable change of style when the real stakes came out, the cry sounded: "Get Dulaney."

Dulaney was a Yankee. He talked in a strange, clipped way the infrequent times he had occasion to let loose, going straight to the point with no fooling around. He had no elaborate greetings, meandering jokes, or lazy style of slouching when he was tired. At times he seemed to dislike every aspect of southern life, and I often wondered why he stuck around in the first place. On the outside he worked as a civil engineer for a government that was laying down highways right and left over farmlands and woods, projects of progress that seemed to hold special appeal for those not particularly caring for the region. They got the chance to cover it in concrete. Often Dulaney came straight to the Buffalo from some dusty stretch of bulldozed earth, wearing boots with loose strings flapping and a windbreaker covered with slate-gray powder. He was a bachelor and ate, as they say, at Mrs. Trivette's boardinghouse. My own family trooped into Mrs. Trivette's for supper now and then, on the heels of my father's hot complaints, my mother and aunt saying it would do us all good to get out in the world and splurge once in awhile; the price, fifty cents a head. It also gave the womenfolk a chance to avoid cooking, my father and I having trouble comprehending why that was such a treat for them. (Our own cooking was having the joy of opening a can of chili beans and heating wienies in boiling water. Nothing to it.) I hated eating around outsiders and being on my best behavior but, as usual, did what I was told.

And generally somewhere among those faces shoveling in the grub was Dulaney—silent, assured with knife and fork the way he was with cue stick, his baldpate taking on a shimmer from the strong overhead light. God, old Dulaney. It made me feel funny to cross paths with him here, among old maid school teachers, chatterbox salesmen, and beaming church leaders, neither of us even nodding to each other and recognizing the roughhouse world of the Buffalo we'd just left. Frankly, he didn't do much nodding to me down at the poolroom either, his aura of aloneness and coolness so complete. And always at Mrs. Trivette's I fought the urge—like the one that beckoned for me to fly out of open windows—to suddenly stand at the table while the jabber went on about the weather and prayer meetings, look Dulaney in the eye, and scream, "The six in the side pocket. *Yaaa hooo!*"

Only at Mrs. Trivette's table did Dulaney seem to feel the necessity for removing his hat. He liked the snap-brim kind with a flashy feather in the ribbon, a plastic cover sheathing the works during a wet day. He wore rimless glasses, was slight of build, and had a narrow, pinched face. Hustlers who showed up at the Buffalo from far and wide soon had the pleasure of meeting him, and Dulaney—to no one's memory —had ever lost to a single one. His reputation held that he would shoot anyone at any time for any sum. It took only a flick of his eye at someone to tell how many points to spot, how much money he could milk out of him, and about how long it would take. He was impatient at all times, as if he had only five minutes left before the train left for back up North. Hat pushed back, eyeballs swiveling up and down above his cue, he sank ball after ball after ball, no shot impossible.

He *had* lost once, we all knew, but that had been to the great Willie Mosconi, pocket billiard champion of the world, who had put on an exhibition at the Buffalo one time as part of a nationwide tour for Brunswick Billiard Tables. Dulaney had removed his hat that evening, sported a bow tie and dark suit, and even looked as if he had greased back the one or two gray hairs on his head. We had all dressed up in our own way for that evening, the great Willie himself, a short man with a good paunch, in a tuxedo and patent-leather slippers. Dulaney introduced Willie in a short formal speech, turning beet red, dignified applause resounding—except from Humphrey who yelled, "Eat shit, fuckface," and was chased out—and then the two men fell into a snappy game that was over, Willie's favor, before anyone knew it. Immediately Willie was off to another town, champions not able to stand still. But before he left, he had said, tapping Dulaney's shoulder, "This fellow is some shot."

Now the man who had played the great Willie Mosconi came up to Pancho. If Pancho was to keep playing, not ready to take home his spoils yet, then he must take on the person ranked above Curly. It wouldn't do to grub anymore for nickels and dimes with some country boy off the streets. The rules called for it. He must play Dulaney, with the rooster feather in his hat, rimless glasses, and ice-blue eyes. And Dulaney had his duty, too, like a fireman called to put out a blaze. Pancho had suddenly risen from the muck of hungry and awkward young players, burning bright, like a rube with straw out the ears who miraculously begins sinking balls when the large money comes out. Dulaney must stamp out Pancho's flame for safety's sake. No long-term, poolroom hustler wanted to believe that a young player, not quite dry behind the ears, could come in and take over. Who would be safe then? The order of the world would be changed.

The two players came to a quick understanding on how many points Pancho should be spotted; a coin sparkled up to see who would break; and a crowd materialized around the table as always happened when Dulaney was shooting. People drifted up to me, astounded. "What's happening? Does Dulaney have to play children now?" I looked at Pancho's old gray sweater, the one he'd worn for years; his black, never-polished shoes I had seen at odd angles in his room those times I had come to wake him up. And here he was now, drawing back on a cue, playing the best in town, going for broke. He won the first game, actually did—more skillful on the final, deciding balls than he was on the earlier runs. All eyes on him, the silence making your groin tight—and still he kept winning. At some point night fell, and I went to the phone to check in with home. Seldom could I ever say truthfully where I was, but some location must be named. The rules, again. "Where are you?" my mother asked. Balls clicked behind me, a Schlitz was being banged down on the counter beside me by the hot dog girl.

"Down at the bowling alley, Mom."

In mid-evening Dulaney started taking games, and those near me began smiling and nodding. Pancho, I wanted to say, just hold on, don't bet so much, you've proved you can shoot with the best. But guess what? Pancho raised the ante—talked Dulaney into shooting for double, twenty dollars a whack. And know what? He turned the tide, began winning once more. Dulaney slipped out one of his infrequent Yankee cuss words, "Jesus K. Rist," and miscued on a sharp side-pocket shot. Pancho stepped up, leaned over, and ran a rack-and-a-half. By the late hours Dulaney was finding fault all around him. The rack boy—eighty-year-old Ted—wasn't moving fast enough; a spectator grazed his elbow on one shot; and cigarette flakes were showing up on the table. "I can't fight all this," he said. He didn't seem to think Pancho himself had anything to do with it; it was circumstances, a conspiracy. "It beats anything I've ever seen. I'm quitting for the night."

"Play one more game, Dulaney. Come on."

"No," bringing out his final, Yankee saying of the evening: "Somebody must have shoved a gold brick up your ass today."

After a farewell pee in the dingy back closet—kicking aside the empty after-shave lotion bottles, which the World War I gas victims housed at the Soldiers' Home, in desperate need of alcohol, had drained back there—I got together with Pancho at the sink where mops were wrung and hands occasionally washed by those who'd just peed. There was a bar of Oxydol soap, and only the cold water tap worked. Pancho was bathing his face and hair in the icy water. He had been bending over the table for over twelve hours now. God, how much had he won, what was he going to do with it? He must be bone weary. "Let's walk home," I said.

"No, I've got enough dough to finally get in that game at the Andrew Jackson. I'm going to see me a few cards tonight."

"You're nuts. Why throw away all the loot so's you can play with those big guys? Son of a bitch, Pancho, those guys make a *living* at poker. They'll kill you."

"Boney, Boney, you don't understand a thing. When you're hot, really hot, you keep going. It's your only chance to win big—and that's all I've ever been interested in. To hell with peanuts."

Back to the phone. "Hello, Mom," after many rings, picturing how she had sidestepped down the stairs in her nightdress to answer, heavy sleep in her eyes. "Listen, I'm going to spend the night at Ghazi's."

"What have you been doing?"

"Oh, being with some of the fellows from school. We've been telling jokes."

"Well, just so long as we know you're in good company."

"I am, Mom. They're really fine guys. See you in the morning."

"Do you want to go to church tomorrow?"

Since I had discovered it wasn't a criminal offense to stay away, I hadn't darkened the door there for the last four years, but every Saturday night she asked that same question. "No, I think I'll skip it tomorrow. Need the sleep, you know. But one of these Sundays I'm going to go. I promise."

"Now, Johnny. You keep saying that."

The Hotel Andrew Jackson was twenty stories high, the town's skyscraper. There the hordes of traveling salesmen stayed, beefy-faced men who strode through the revolving door—the town's only one—shoes burnishing like old furniture, their suits pressed, swinging the satchels of their trade. They talked in strange accents, forever buying papers, asking street directions, hurrying on. A number of rich people in town kept permanent rooms at the Andrew Jackson, tottering down at mealtime to the dining room where the heavy silverware shone, every napkin had a holder, and soft-footed, good-natured black waiters eased up just before the moment you needed something. The hotel's giant second-floor ballroom served for dances, dinners where politicians blathered and congratulated each other, and as a place for visiting celebrities—like Eleanor Roosevelt or an escapee from a Soviet prison camp—to hold forth at a sold-out banquet. The hotel was self-contained, like a ship, having a barbershop, drugstore, and a cavernous lobby, easy chairs and deep sofas all over, where a radio blared at every important occasion, like a World Series game, a presidential speech, or Amos 'n' Andy.

The Andrew Jackson was so high that a sure suicide could be had from leaping off the top; none of the three- and four-storied buildings around could guarantee it so emphatically. Once a prominent man in town, part of the Pine Crest enclave, sailed off the roof around the noon hour, thoughtfully aiming himself at a seldom-used back alley. He had just served as best man in a wedding, saying after the reception that he just wanted to stop in the hotel a moment for a pack of butts. Everyone said he was in high, good spirits. Through the revolving door he had gone from a waiting, purring car —and was next seen heading for the concrete. Who could understand it? The local paper ran a photograph of the Andrew Jackson with an arrow showing his path, but they could find no reason for it other than his mother had been in poor health. Could we ever be sure of what went on in the heads of those we saw every day?

Bellhops at the Andrew Jackson wore tunics with brass buttons and trousers with stripes up the side—not like LeRoy over at the Dixie with his squashed cap and pokey gait. Pancho caught the portly, exquisitely mannered one by the elevator, a leader in the black community along with the funeral home director, his name in the paper a lot. "Where's the game tonight?" Pancho said.

"Which one?"

"The biggest. The one Floyd Waters is in."

"Hop in, I'll take you up." And as the machine hummed, added, looking straight ahead at the gate, "Can I get you boys a little drinking whiskey?"

"Yeah. A pint of Four Roses." Pancho gave him a dollar more than he asked for. Man.

Only one or two heads turned when we entered the room. A slim, gray-haired man—a postman, I remembered—was the only man to smile, a forced, unhappy one. "You boys can take my place after this hand," he said. "I'm snakebit." He did lose, looking disgustingly at his cards, throwing money up in the air toward the pot. It made me sad, just thinking of a postman gambling in the first place. They were supposed to be carrying the mail. A swarthy man I'd seen striding in and out

183

of the poolroom with his nose up acted as a sort of host for the game. He wore strange clothes for our town, like something Perry Como might choose: suede shoes and a turtleneck shirt within a green, zippered sweater. He took fifty cents from each pot for room costs and management, a representative for one of the many things that went on behind closed doors in Our Town. Behind a door that said, "Private, No Admittance," in a downtown hamburger joint—flocks going in and out—was a giant room everybody knew about with ticker tape sputtering, the latest baseball results being chalked up, and money changing hands as a result of tiny slips gouged from punchboards. Once a nice, respectful boy in high school had drawn the winning number from the punchboard and had shyly gone to the place's owner, a banty rooster of a man who liked to stand on a raised platform by the baseball returns. "Son," the grown man had said, stuffing the winning ticket in his pocket, "you're too young to be gambling. I won't tell the police this time, but next time I might. I'm letting you off."

"Thanks a lot, sir," the nice boy had said. "I sure do appreciate that."

Under trap doors of frame houses scattered throughout town were liquor caches, a man in overalls or a granny or sometimes a child going for your order when you drove up in back or slipped up quietly on the front porch. At liquor referendum time, everybody understood, the bootleggers and the Baptist ministers would always defeat the measure. *Look* magazine had voted Our Town an Honorable Mention in its list of the most crime-infested cities in the nation. All of us had been tremendously pleased with that honor, though worried that there might be some kind of crime in town we were missing out on.

The Big Card Game kept moving—in a motel for awhile,

the back room of the hamburger joint, now in the Andrew Jackson. Pancho took a seat, and placed a stack of bills before him since chips were not used. The game was five-card stud, and the sky was the limit. He dropped out quickly on the first several hands, as if he might be hesitant on exactly what to do. I moved around, sitting on the bed a moment, then leaning to peek when Pancho wanted to show me what he had in the hole. Frankly, I wasn't too sure how poker was played, my main knowledge coming from cowboy movies and a brief instruction once from Uncle Buford when he'd been drinking. Hearts played on a rainy afternoon was my speed. But I nodded gravely at the hole card, letting everyone know I was buddies with one of the Big Game players. Get a load of me, guys. And maybe if Pancho won, we could order up two girls in a flourish from the bellhop to let everybody know we could fuck. Pancho took a sip of Four Roses, wiped the back of his hand across his lips, and didn't take his eyes from the game.

His stack of bills went steadily down, all that money he had won so painstakingly from Curly and Dulaney. He would have a promising card or two showing and then someone would bet a fortune—usually Floyd Waters—and Pancho would drop out and pull his nose. Floyd, in a plum-colored silk shirt, had few words until he raked in a large pot. Then: "Boys, I'm going to rupture my cuzzy this way pretty soon. Come to papa, baby." His Tennessee accent, just like a regular person's, sounded odd at such times, your expecting some sort of fluting, God-like voice to ease from between his purple lips. During a brief span in the war, he had belonged to the merchant marines and had swung down from a train on occasion at the depot in what looked like an admiral's uniform. He would then amble to a pay phone in the newsstand—all kids' eyes on him—and, opening a little black book as they did in the movies, call someone. To be able to do *that!* How could Pancho hope to come even near whipping such a man?

"How's your Uncle Buford?" he said, seeming to notice Pancho for the first time.

"Aw, fine."

"I'll tell you this about Buford Johnson. He's going to run them communists out of Nashville." By "communists" he meant Democrats who voted for a minimum wage. "And who's that long drink of water over there?" I told him, and he immediately got me mixed up with a family in town who ran a flower shop. I didn't try to correct him, and laughed as much as anyone when he asked how the weather was up my way. I'd heard that one before. But you tended to smile a lot around Floyd Waters—even when he stepped on your foot down at the poolroom or poked you in the gut on a shot. It was as if it was your fault in the first place, to be in his way. But all laughing stopped suddenly.

Pancho raised Floyd with two cards showing, then pulled his nose. He had just been dealt an eight, a queen beside it. Floyd had a ten and king up, and raised right back. Everybody dropped out but Pancho. What the hell did he have? I leaned down for a squint, but he wasn't showing. He had just looked at the hidden card once himself, that was all. The other cards that were now dealt seemed about as inappropriate as you could get for such a high-level game—a three and six for Pancho, a deuce and seven for Floyd, colors mixed. But they kept raising back and forth as if they held royal straight flushes. Finally, after two raises on the last card, Floyd Waters took a fat billfold, studied the bills inside a long, long while, and said, "Tell you what, little Buford. I think I'll just bump you back a little old hundred bucks. Come on, call. See what I got in the hole."

"Please, Pancho," I said, leaning down. He nodded—and I bent up the corner of his hidden card. An ace. Son of a bitch. Not even a pair. At least I knew that much about poker. All Floyd Waters needed was a measly pair to win. Surely a man who flew to the Kentucky Derby and didn't wear pockets on the back of his britches would have a pair.

"Call," Pancho said. He turned his front pockets inside out, watch pocket, went through his shirt's breast pocket, and borrowed five dollars and some change from me with a strict promise he'd pay me back tomorrow if he lost—which I was certain he would. But he came up with a hundred dollars. Down it went. Then he and Floyd looked each other in the eye—for what seemed a good minute or so. Floyd's expression changed first.

"Beat it," he said, pointing to the king. In the hole he had a jack.

Pancho turned over the ace. "Excuse me, pardon me," he said, drawing in money with both hands, chortling in his playing-dirty style.

He kept winning after that, phenomenally so. Floyd Waters said nothing, his expression as cool as a cucumber. What a sport. Finally, though, came the hand where Pancho nosed out Floyd's three queens with a jack-high straight, taking the biggest pot of the evening. Floyd stood quite calmly, like a preacher about to lead a hymn, then grabbed a whiskey glass and threw it against the wall. "Of all the goddamn fucking shit! Don't you know enough to fold! You drew out on me!"

By the time Pancho and I trotted back out the revolving door, no one was on the street. The air had a crisp, unreal scent, as if we were being born into something new, making me feel so good I thought about throwing a brick through Liggett's plate-glass window. Nothing could go wrong, ever. A car-pool comrade was snoring on the couch when we got to the Sheik's, so Pancho and I grabbed blankets from the closet to roll up Indian-style on the floor, as the Boy Scouts had taught us. But first he sat cross-legged beneath a lamp turned on low, pulling crumpled bills from his pockets and ironing them out with his thumb before placing them in stacks. He mumbled under his breath, sweating at the addition, not glancing at me. It was the way we used to play Monopoly. He made ten stacks, a hundred dollars in each. *A thousand bucks!* "How did you do it? You didn't have a thing this morning."

"Boney, there are times when you know you can't lose. A gambler milks them times dry."

"Listen, buy a car—and let me drive it some. Why not?"

"No, I don't think so. I'm going to really use this dough."

He hadn't even bought me a hamburger, and I'd been by his side all day. Pancho, sensing my thoughts, began buttering me up with the usual. I would help him on an English theme and a chemistry assignment, make sure his grades were good enough for him to graduate. And then he began the new track, which he'd started using more and more recently, about how I was certain to make it to Europe some day. Translated, he was telling me that I was destined for higher plateaus than he was: his way of a compliment. Promise you'll take me with you, he said. Just promise, that's all. Usually this would have been enough to soften me. But not this time. Down in my heart I was a little resentful that he had beaten everybody and proved to be a winner once more. How come I had to lose so often?

It was only possible for me to nod off that night, never being able to really sleep away from home, coming awake when I heard Pancho shifting the loot from one hiding place on himself to another. Who knew what thieves might barge in and roll him? The Sheik passed through at dawn in a pair of tentlike drawers, scratching his armpit and breaking wind before raiding the icebox. He growled something about Pancho freeloading once again. . . .

Pancho still kept taking Meredith out on the occasions you would expect people "going steady" to honor, Friday nights and to the infrequent parties. He was his normal stiff self then, opening doors, guiding her along by the elbow, mumbling words. His face was pale those times under his dark hair, as if he might be in the grips of a migraine. When the yearbook, bound in red, imitation leather, came hot off the presses into our hands one sunny spring day, I fought with myself through four classes before working up courage to suddenly thrust my copy under Meredith's nose in chemistry lab. Her eyes widened and she sucked in her breath till her mouth formed an O, as if my yearbook was the one she looked most forward to scribbling in. She wrote in a clear, even hand, "You're one of my very, very favorites, Johnny, and I'll always remember you. Don't ever forget The Long Walk. It was fun, though."

Then her precious yearbook came into my hands. Already it was crammed full of signatures and messages, even Jujube the janitor having gotten something in there ahead of me. I took out my Sheaffer and wrote quickly because the damn thing leaked, "Meredith, don't take any wooden nickels or forget your cheerleading yells. How come we're all so nuts about you?" It didn't seem to make much sense, but it was all I knew to write. I had memorized it.

Pancho and I exchanged messages because everyone else was doing it, as if we didn't expect to keep seeing each other after graduation. Where were we going to go, though? He borrowed my pen and wrote, "Boney, you sure aire a louscy pool shot. Best o lucke!" Then he did a curious thing, drawing an arrow to the picture of Meredith's beaming, nice face. By it he added, "Woemin aire goen to kill us someday, waite and see."

The girl who was always edging beside me in physics tore my yearbook out of my hands and started writing until I thought she'd never stop, filling a whole back page. I'd only put a line in hers. Then, smiling insanely—which surely she was—she turned and fled down the hall. "You never pay any attention to me," she yelled, over her shoulder. "You don't know what you're missing!" I tried to find the qualities I'd missed as her legs whipped back and forth. She had good calves, her soft brown hair bounced nicely, and there was some evidence of breasts, I noted, as she turned the corner. What was wrong? In my yearbook she had recorded all high-lights from our physics class, plus every encounter we'd had in the cafeteria and on the stairs. She was petulant about my not speaking to her once on the street. I must have been in a daze then and only overlooked her. She had more than one com-plaint, though, noting even how I sang off-key in assembly. It was hard to tell what would satisfy her except my being en-tirely different. Then why was she taken so much with me in the first place?

The weather grew warmer, summerish, and then there was no holding it back any longer—son of a bitch, we graduated.

The orchestra played "Pomp and Circumstance," and we came down the aisle in the gym on the beat. We wore rented mortarboards and black gowns that smelled heavily of the drycleaners, and—grown-up eyes on us—felt proud and ri-diculous at the same time. The commencement address was given by a tall, flabby man in glasses. It had something to do with America the Beautiful, a better world—matters that caused several heads to loll. The only way I could stay awake was to picture myself coming back twenty-five years later to address another graduating class. I'd be dressed sharp, and I'd let both barrels off at the beginning. "Gang," I'd say, "I know what's bothering you out there because I've been there myself. You're worried about what you'll ever be able to do in the outside world," looking off at my fifth wife, a mixture of Meredith Lancaster and a movie star, "but let me tell you that whatever it is, it'll be a damn sight better than what you've just left. Pardon the French," eying the red-faced principal, the same one as now. "And let me close by saying that I wish every graduating girl would now lie back, raise her gown, and let those of us on stage have a squint of her pussy. Thank you, and good night."

After a series of backbreaking prayers, our names were called, in alphabetical order, and we proceeded on stage to take a rolled diploma tied with a red ribbon and shake the commencement speaker's big hand. (We were warned beforehand not to cause a squawk if we got the wrong sheepskin; we could exchange them later outside.) On the stage we marched, tossing the mortarboard tassel from one side to the other as we completed the process, the mark of a graduate. The only one to get a laugh was Jack Renfrew, a section-eight vet from the army. His name still echoing through the steel rafters, he strode on stage, clicked his heels before the dignitaries and saluted the commencement speaker as if he were General George S. Patton. A smart left face, and then he forward-marched off stage, having trouble keeping his mortarboard on because, for some kind of imagined military requirement, he had recently shaved his head as bald as a bullet. Sights such as Jack Renfrew made you think twice about rushing out to join the armed services.

Gowns off, diplomas handed over to loved ones, we went off to celebrate as best we knew how. A cousin and his wife drove me over to the American Legion Hall, where a dance was being held, because I didn't have a date and was too embarrassed to bum a ride with a buddy who did; for instance, with Pancho, who rattled off beside Meredith in Uncle Buford's V-8. My arms folded against the back of the front seat, watching my cousin steer carefully down a side road, I said, "Boy oh boy, no more school. Now my troubles are really over. . . ." My cousin and his wife both turned around, looked silently at me, and then faced forward.

We knew this graduation dance was special because we told each other so—feeling it was the last time we'd ever get together en masse quite this way. Otherwise, it was a lot like any other dance. Humphrey got tossed out the first half-hour for goosing a chaperon's wife. There were two fights, not counting the one that Humphrey put up. I danced four times with Meredith, and after the last one asked if she'd like to step out on the terrace for a breath of fresh air. Only, after having hugged her perfumed body for the length of "Slow Boat to China," it came out, "A *bed* of fresh air." She took it for just another one of my convoluted witticisms, saying, "Yes, I'd just love a bed of fresh air."

We sat on cold stones, myself pretending to rock to the music but actually trying to keep my butt from freezing. Why were we only together under the harshest of physical conditions—in a cramped back seat, on a long walk, my neck swiveling around at a school desk, now my ass on an iceberg? What would have happened if we could have lay in deep cushions around a scented, Romanesque bath? Here we looked at the stars, congratulated each other once again on graduating, and babbled about tomorrow. I told her I was thinking about thumbing around the country this coming summer, maybe down to Florida. I wouldn't, but it sounded good.

Meredith said, "I'm going to start college this summer."

"What's the rush?"

"My mother wants me to. And Daddy, too. I can't wait."

When I wasn't cutting in on Meredith on the floor, I stood by the soft-drink stand and watched others do their numbers with her. Here came the big, wide-eyed greeting to first one, then another. But in Pancho's arms she rested her head studiedly on his shoulder, the time for all-out greetings over. And he then put his cheek against her brown-blonde hair, a little too much the devoted suitor, a near chuckle on his lips. In a certain light he reminded me of John Barrymore, the Great Profile, still playing boudoir scenes in his late movies but letting you know that this time he was in on the joke; probably had a snoutful in him then, too, if you could believe the legend. And it wasn't unlikely that Pancho might have been lifting some Four Roses himself on his trips to the john. He walked very carefully, holding his head high, acting more sober than necessary.

After "Goodnight, Sweetheart," people piled in cars, calling others to join them. There were all-night parties to be held in a farm outside of town and in a summer house by the lake. I waved off this and that car, inhaling their exhausts, too ashamed to admit that I was not only without a date, but without transportation. Girls flashed their thighs as they lifted a foot toward back seats; boys sat seriously erect in the driver's seat. Ernie Peoples called to me several times—Did I have a ride? Which one of the parties was I heading for? He'd have to throw a headlock to get me in his back seat. I didn't want his charity.

Finally, out of the whole graduation class I stood alone in the American Legion parking lot. Walking the five miles home, I threw up images of what the parties would be like. I could see Meredith sitting on the floor, her long legs tucked under her, phonograph music blaring beside her. I saw people jitterbugging and trucking on down, maybe some advanced guy getting a feel in a locked bedroom. Blindfolded I could have made my way home, so well did I know every rut and curve that led there. My bed had been freshly made by my mother and I swam my arms and legs around sensuously on the clean, sun-scented sheets before dropping off.

In the morning the first thing I heard was that Ernie Peoples had been in an automobile accident. Floorboarding down Main Street on the way to the party, an arm wrapped around Sally Jane, gabbing with someone in the back seat, his trick knee had locked on the gas, and, quietly informing his passengers of that fact, had expertly dodged an oncoming car, only to sail while they screamed like banshees through the plate-glass window of Liggett's, through the candy counter and magazine rack and lipstick display, coming to a rest with front wheels over the soda fountain. From a hospital bed—his leg in traction, his hugging arm bent in plaster—he told me again and again how he had swerved around the car in front, dwelling on every detail, the one thing he had to be proud of. He said the ride inside Liggett's had happened so fast he couldn't remember details, seeming terribly embarrassed for a change himself.

Down at the poolroom we all mulled over the details Ernie couldn't remember, marveling at the fact that everyone had got out without a terribly serious injury. Right into Liggett's like a cannonball. It gave us something to talk about and consider for the first few days after graduation at least. Now there were no classes to jump up for in the mornings, and the summer didn't stretch out as a bridge between school years anymore. What to do? I talked to an army recruiter, who made the service seem like a Florida vacation. A downtown store owner cornered me one day, telling me he thought I had great potential for selling refrigerators and stoves. I would go around knocking on strange doors, charming the people inside into giving the stuff a try. He pulled out reams of company material, which favored a lot of diagrams of large shoe prints trudging up to stick houses and some dialogue between Mr. Homeowner and Mr. Salesman. The mere thought of such life work caused the world around to go dim. What I did was hang around the poolroom through the waking hours. Pancho would come by a short time after breakfast, and we'd be off.

One day he was late, and had an odd smile when I came out jauntily snapping the screen door shut behind me. It was a sneaky, pained smile, like a gunfighter's right before he draws. There was hate in it. "You've got to loan me a few bucks today, Boney."

"Loan *you* money? Are you crazy? What happened to the thousand?"

"Awww." He turned his head, hands in pockets. His voice now had no edge or bite, no game to play, resigned to the truth. "I gave the money to my mother to put in the bank for me, and guess what she did? She gave it to Thaddeus. My old man."

"You're kidding. Your mother? A mother just wouldn't do that."

"Boney, she's a woman. You've lived too sheltered a life. You don't understand."

"But why'd you have to tell her about the money? Why didn't you put it in the bank yourself? God almighty, Pancho."

"Awww," the edge still missing to his voice, "I wanted to impress her, I guess, show her how I'd done something big and important. And then I got suckered in. It felt so good . . . trusting her. . . ."

"Is it *all* gone? Every bit?"

"Every last nickel. She cried and said Thaddeus was sick and had desperately needed it. Sick, shit. Drunk. She promised that I'd get the money back soon—in a year, sometime. It's gone, though. Kaput. Her promises and a nickel will get you a Coca-Cola."

A memory passed through my mind which I couldn't tell Pancho about. Once I had been ambling down Main Street in my usual dazed state, fired up by having just memorized some garter-revealing poses from *Life,* gratis the railroad newsstand counter, when a woman's heart-shaped bottom in a tight skirt suddenly flashed before me in reality. Hypnotized, I followed it down Main, up Thompson for a block or two, and then into the coffee shop in the Andrew Jackson. At the soda fountain its owner turned, and it was Pancho's mother. I was mortified, not sure what new depths my lust had now driven me. Incest? I tried to erase what I'd felt on watching her bottom wiggle and see her once more as just Pancho's mom. She was a pretty, sandy-haired woman who might have been beautiful in her prime. She joked with a salesclerk, seeming scatterbrained in fumbling with her change while buying something. Her purse snapped shut, a cheery nod to all and sundry, she dashed back out as if there were a myriad happy things left to be done in the world. Every time I'd ever seen her she had been cheerful—and jittery. There was the time on Uncle Buford's front porch when she had playfully mussed Pancho's hair—already growing thin—saying, "Oh, look at my sad old boy. He's turning into the biggest fuddy duddy in town. He's just got to have some fun!"

Pancho's dad was of course barred from Uncle Buford's, taking cover in neighboring towns and only making brief forays into the back streets of town. I would see him on occasion in a Market Street beer joint, sitting by himself at the counter, dark like Pancho—seeming angry at something unspecified, ready to throw a bottle or two. He was barred from a few of the joints, too.

"Well, listen, Pancho," I said, trying to cheer him up, "it was just gambling money. You can win some more."

"Yeah, sure, you bet." We crossed the tracks in the heart of town, turning right for the Buffalo. All at once Pancho stopped dead and turned to me. His jaw muscles were working, his jugular pronounced, a broken smile—and I felt guilty, I didn't know why. "Boy, you're a lucky bastard. You've always had a real home and everything."

Yes, home would always be there. The rituals would continue forever, the fabric so strong; unthinkable otherwise. Right after supper my father would shoo away whoever was on the couch—often me—and then, resting his head on a newspaper over a cushion, sleep until time to depart for the depot. A light might shine in his face, bellows ricochet in the hall, and yet he would be sawing logs right up to the last minute, waking in good humor, with, "Hey, look what time it is. Mother, have you got my lunch box ready?"

"Yes, Tom," my mother would always say, not looking up from the book she was reading.

On cold mornings my mother would wake me, and I would stand in pajamas over the hot-air register, lazily coming to life, while my eggs or whatever I'd ordered were being fixed. And then from on high, at approximately eight fifteen, would come the standard, window-rattling shout from my Aunt Milly: "Somebody open the George door! I'm coming down!" No one knew why she called the front door the "George door"; she couldn't explain it either.

"But, Aunt Milly," I would scream, "it'll freeze us to death. You're not even in sight yet."

She had a job to go to, and Miss Thelma Mahoney would have just pulled up outside in her 1932 Chevvy, her first honk resounding.

"Willie, Chip, the door, the door." Here she came down the steps, clomp clomp, knees out. "Sug Willie, Sug Willie!" I was called by so many names that the FBI was never going to figure out who I really was when it came time to investigate me. I would open the door, feeling an arctic blast take away all the work the furnace had put in my bones, and then I would jump aside. My aunt would fly past, flattening the screen out with the side of her arm, her scarf trailing in the breeze. It would be then left to me to go bent-over to rebarricade the door.

My mother would always be around to pour milk at meals, jumping up to fill my glass every time it was down below the halfway mark. Jack Benny would come on the air at seven sharp Sunday night, the "Hit Parade" at nine on Saturday. We had a radio at last, a marvelous Silvertone from Sears and Roebuck, perched on a wobbly table I'd made in Manual Training. Like all mechanical things it soon developed its own eccentricities. To get a low rumble from its speaker changed into something intelligible you had to smack it hard on the side in just a certain way. My father and I became very adept at this chore, sort of liking it, my mother and aunt never able to come close. They didn't like the radio anyhow, preferring to be near warmth and the nineteenth century. The Silvertone was always placed near a drafty window. To bring in faraway stations, like Cincinnati where "One Man's Family" came from, someone—me—had to hold the live-end of a short wire marked "antenna." It would probably have been easier to install an ordinary outside antenna and be done with it, but that would have been fully committing ourselves to the twentieth century. It would have been admitting that the radio was there to stay; it seemed my mother and aunt were just waiting for those tremendous smacks of ours not to work and then the toy would be thrown out. Back to the classics, everybody.

Before the radio came my mother used to entertain me by playing the piano. The heavy upright stood in the front bedroom—the "Crumb Room," my aunt called it. For awhile during my nomadic life through the house I slept in the Crumb Room. From the bed, wanting just the right touch before surrendering to sleep, I would call, "Momma, play just one song for me. Please!"

She would leave *Decline of the West,* place marked, and seat herself on the broken piano stool. (My big brother had spilled some liniment on it while his bare foot was up on it, treating an athletic injury, and the medicine had eaten off layers of varnish, too.) My mother liked to play hymns at first, those she had learned in childhood. "The Old Rugged Cross" and "I Walk Through the Garden Alone." She would sing a chorus or two, and I would hum along, turning on my side to watch her stamping the pedals, her fingers flying over the yellowed keyboard, face lifted. When she began to turn over sheet after sheet of music, a sign of weariness, I pleaded, "Momma, play some of the other songs. Come on. Please. Just a few."

She played songs that had been current from around the turn of the century and during the First World War—yet more evocative to me than anything on the "Hit Parade."

> *Oh, the moon shines tonight*
> *on pretty Red Wing,*
> *The breeze is sighing,*
> *My heart is crying. . . .*

When she did "It's a Long, Long Way to Tipperary," I kind of marched in bed, swinging my head from side to side, a doughboy off to war. With "Smile Awhile," I tingled all over in comfort and happiness because my mother put a cheerful, graceful lilt to the bittersweet lyrics. Finally, though, came the time—after "Jerusalem, Jerusalem," "She's Only a Bird in a Gilded Cage," and "Red Wing" once more on request—when she closed the music sheets and rose. "We'll play them again some time," she'd say. "Now go to sleep."

My big older brother would always be coming home on a visit from some distant, glamorous spot, tall and curly haired, stepping off the train in naval officer braid or wheeling up in a convertible. It was impossible to ever consider being near his equal, but I could devise intricate ways of just being noticed by him. Once when his cronies filled the living room— smoking, spinning service yarns—I came in and said I'd learned a new wrestling hold and would like to try it out on him. All right, he said, but make it snappy. Everything I did around him always had to be snappy, timed to perfection. It was a jujitsu hold I had picked up from Humphrey who had picked it up from a relative who was a U.S. Ranger. In a flash, taking my brother's hand and throwing a foot out, I had him down on the floor screaming. His cronies whooped. "God almighty damn," he bellowed, wringing his arm, when I finally let loose. "You could kill somebody with that hold. Don't ever do that again, you fool!"

"O.K.," I said, marching upstairs, head high. Inside my room I beat my head as quietly as possible against the wall and cried. He'd called me a fool. And he'd always know how to make me feel like one.

My father would keep smoking two packs of Chesterfields through infinity. The aroma seeped into my sweaters, the drapes, the very woodwork of the house. In my brother's memory, before my time, was a picture of my father being a manager of the local baseball team. He had gloried more in winning and had taken losses harder than anyone he had ever known, my brother remembered. Once my dad had played the game himself—catcher, disdaining a mask in order to see better, fearless. They said he could have gone to the major leagues if it hadn't been for "throwing his arm away" one spring through overzealousness. Now, a short time after arising in the afternoon, he walked downtown to catch the latest game results, saying he was going for a Coke. I caught him once or twice raising a brew downtown when he thought he was safe in some side joint—and loved him for it. He would always be around to give me advice on drinking, though. And on everything else, too. You could count on that.

It was all part of family, a million vibrations and smells and rituals. It was all I had ever known, and I couldn't conceive of it ending or changing radically. It would have been like imagining death. My mother, though, had tried to enlarge my world at every opportunity: the Sunday *Times* in the mailbox, trips to Knoxville to hear world leaders, countless encouragements to learn about the outside. It was up to me to take those first steps away, but Home would always be there to come back to. That was the feeling. Yes, Pancho was right about my having a real home. And I felt terribly smug and secure. Later, I would have known that this mood might be a warning buzzer for a crash. For nothing that is alive in this world—person as well as idea—is ever safe.

My mother left. She got a job running a gift shop. Swift as that. One minute she was always home; the next she was at the store all day and tired and sleepy at night. It was the prelude to when she would not be there at all, when all there was was memory. We ate out at boardinghouses, our names garbled, dutifully carrying our plates to the sink when finished in order to keep in good standing with the landlady. The meals were cheap, but not everyone welcome from town. The breakfast plates at our house were now washed by my father—with help from me, an unemployed, when he could corral me. Just when I'd be settled back with the Drama Section of *The New York Times,* my guard down, he'd spring. "Come on, hot shot. Let's tackle these plates." We both donned aprons, which looked like napkins attached to our six-foot-three frames, and then dug in, causing suds and water to splash on floor, ceiling, and walls. The process seemed to carry into eternity, coffee grounds clogging the drain, a dirty bowl discovered after we'd thought we were through, a glass broken and a hand bleeding. Sometimes I escaped by creeping out the door at the sound of his step and a cigarette cough, flying downtown to the pool-room until the danger period passed. But then guilt would strike, my hand miscuing, thinking about him plowing through the debris, washing and drying *both*. I would hurry back at the tail end to do at least one or two plates, cleansing my conscience to boot.

My father did not seem displeased that my mother was now working. He hugged and kissed her more often these days, embarrassing us all, and made little jokes about her prowess. She certainly was a dynamo at the gift shop, her first job away from home in some thirty-odd years. Well into the night she'd often be tying up loose strings, getting deliveries made to some outlying house, listening woefully to complaints. If no other way was available for a must delivery, she would trudge herself a mile or two to make it. If not her—due to exhaustion—then me. Through a rainstorm, no umbrella, I carried a card and a box of chocolates under my shirt to a home in the Pine Crest Addition on emergency orders. An anniversary had to be honored. The face at the door was obscured, and a hand darted through the crack for the package. My mother would have flown with a fifteen-cent card to

Paris, I'm sure, if someone had needed it. She lost weight, becoming quick and sparrowlike, her face very pale. She became a new person, someone I knew I should get acquainted with. But I missed the old person so.

And I remembered that she had once been still another person—one I'd never hope to know—a young girl my own age. She had been a school teacher then, and, once out of the blue, she had told me a little bit about it. She had made $15 a month, and her room and board had been $12. She had been hungry most of the time because the landlady, the only one in the village, had skimped on meals, my mother having always paid in advance. Lunch had been a piece of cold ham between a hard biscuit. She never said much about her teaching, but it must have been good. Never in my memory had I gone to her with a word whose definition and derivation she didn't know; never an algebra or geometry problem she couldn't unravel. Teachers said I'd go far in math. Left to myself I hardly knew the multiplication table.

And now, left to my own devices, I went to interview after interview, becoming terrified every time someone came close to hiring me. This wasn't like looking for one of those old part-time jobs—the summer and after-school ones—where you could immediately look forward to quitting. Here everything was taken so seriously, a shirt and tie on an interview, and there was no telling when you could escape if taken on. And so, in my gloom, I didn't notice the abrupt fall Pancho was taking. He was just old Pancho, a buddy who could take care of himself, what the hell. He began losing in pool. Bad. His aiming hand shook, and he took chances where his skill wasn't strong enough to back it up. Curly beat him. The first time they played after the famous thousand-dollar Saturday was close—Curly extra cautious, a little tight, Pancho lucky but not lucky enough. The second game Curly won more easily, smiling now, not studying his shots so much. By the time Pancho was down to his last dollar, though, Curly was shooting behind his back and making double bank shots. Finally, Pancho flipped a half a dollar on the table. "O.K., one last one for this."

"Nope," Curly said, unscrewing his stick for the case with the metal snaps, "I don't shoot for pocket change."

He never got to shoot Dulaney again, his bankroll not allowing him championship play. Besides, Curly had put him in his place so why should Dulaney trouble himself? Pancho did play poker again—and Floyd Waters couldn't take his money fast enough, what there was of it. "Come on, boy," Floyd said, "ain't you got no more money than this? You better run home and get some off your Uncle Buford if you want to play real live poker."

For awhile I was still carried by the euphoria of the thousand-dollar day. It would happen again, why not? He would even have a day soon that would top that, surely. He had shown so much promise. But, no. It was like those spectacular football passes he had caught, topping what anyone had done before. You'd have thought he would have gone on to further games, much bigger ones. But that was it. The thousand-dollar day had been the pinnacle of his success, not the dawn of more glories. And it took me awhile to accept it. He came by my house, as always, and I loaned him money. "Boney, look. Maybe I can't shoot the eyes out of 'em anymore. O.K. And poker you got to wait around for the right cards to play. But I know the game where I can take 'em all. Craps. You know how I can tell when I got a hot streak. You seen it. Loan me a couple of bucks, and I swear I'll double it for you today."

The game went on beside the men's room in a beer joint by the railroad tracks. A gang of men and boys hunkered down, some on one knee, the dice clicking off a whitewashed cinderblock wall. "Come on, baby. *Little Joe from Kokomo!"* It seemed so easy—when you had that hot streak. Make the seven or eleven. If not, make your point. All sorts of pleas and rituals were tried to charm the dice. One man—an ex-combat flier for the navy—liked to rub the cubes on his balls before slinging them out, but had to stop when the next shooter always demanded new dice. Pancho won much more than he lost in fading others—causing my hopes to rise—and then his turn came to take the bones. He had passed on two prior occasions, claiming he hadn't felt "hot."

Now he massaged the dice up and down between his palms, shook them next to his ear, blew on them, and then let them sail with a snap of his fingers. I concentrated on a seven in my mind—come on, seven. He hit an eleven. Winner! "Let it all ride, boys, I'm hot," he said. He shook them again, as if jacking off, and then threw them forward. It was a four. "Don't worry, Boney, I told you I was hot. *Come on, four, don't be a whore!"* He kept landing near craps, hitting a six, nine, eight. Then he got well away—snake eyes—and I let my breath out. Then two deuces: a four. A winner once more! Now we were going to have another big day, I thought. Why had I had such little faith? There must have been forty dollars down there in a pile. "Who's going to fade me? I'm leaving it all down." A ten was covered, a five—soon all the money was faded. He massaged the dice as before, shook them as before, everything the same ritual and prayer, and then slung them out. And hit boxcars. He lost it all.

Somewhere along the line I became less ready to run outside when Pancho dropped by now. And there became fewer reasons to stroll down his way. I had *War and Peace* to read, for one thing. Once he yelled up to my second-story window at the usual time, but I lay flat, Tolstoy resting on my belly. Napoleon was about to abandon Moscow in flames. And down below my father was warming up to do the dishes. *"Boney, Boney!"* Why couldn't I have just five or ten minutes to get Napoleon on his way? My father couldn't hear Pancho, not if he had fired a cannon, because my father's hearing was now failing. It used to be that he could catch the sound of my tiptoeing away from every appointed chore. No more. People had to yell at him down at the train station to get his attention —and sometimes that wouldn't even work—and I had a current nightmare of his letting two locomotives collide because he hadn't heard them coming. *"Boney, Boney!"* I turned on my side, and peeked between the curtains. Pancho was strolling away, hands in pockets, his shoulders hunched in. Shit. I dog-eared my place, and went out the side door to catch up with him. A buddy was a buddy.

But Pancho knew that I was less than enthralled about the poolroom these days, that my mind had begun to wander when he told the latest about the Sheik or Uncle Buford, that I might be developing interests other than his own. He then played his trump card, something guaranteed to grab my attention and show that he was still one up on me no matter how many Tolstoys I read. It was the way Ernie Peoples— when he wanted me to hang out with him and I was growing weary—used to describe what his big sister's cunt looked like in the bathtub. I would have followed him to the ends of the earth to have heard the details. And now on one of those evenings when Pancho had Uncle Buford's house to himself for some reason, he called me down and told me to listen in on the extension phone, he had someone he was going to call. I could tell he was excited by the way his jugular stood out, and that triggered my own excitement. I pulled the second-floor extension phone by its long cord down the stairs, and Pancho met me with the hall phone. We both sat, me a couple of steps above him. He called the girls' college in South Carolina and got a dormitory that went by the name of Apple Blossom Hall. "Meredith Lancaster, please," he said, and winked up at me.

"Hello . . . Yes," she said, after an interminable period of nothing.

"It's me, kid."

"Pancho!"

He winked again my way. "Are you missing me a little bit?"

"Yes . . . sure. Pancho, there's so much *homework* to do here. Goodness gracious, it's not at all like high school. And there are girls here from all over. *Yankees* even. We have to——"

"What'a ya think of Boney?"

"Hunh? What are you talking about, Pancho?"

"I mean, what's your opinion of him?"

"He's nice. Quiet. Just a boy. Pancho . . . you're not drinking, are you? You shouldn't, you shouldn't!"

"Listen, kid, have I rubbed your stomach before? Yes or no?"

"Pancho, you just shouldn't talk that way on the phone. No telling who could be listening in someplace. . . . *Listen,* there's a military college twenty miles from here. They have all these rules about our not even nodding to these boys. It's so funny. Can you believe it?"

"Meredith, just admit it. Have I rubbed your stomach, touched you?"

". . . yes, you have, Pancho."

"And are you going to let me do it again?"

". . . if you want to."

"O.K.," the dirty chuckle sounding, "I just wanted you to admit it."

"Oh, Pancho, you're going to make me cry! Why do you always have to be so mean and spoil everything?"

"Because I wasn't brought up any better, I reckon. Keep your legs together, kid."

"Pancho!"

"So long."

He was still into his dirty chuckle as he replaced the receiver and looked up at me. From the bright overhead light I could see the ever-increasing spaces between the black hairs on top of his head. I walked home, picturing Meredith breathless at the dormitory phone, intermixed with shots of how Pancho's hand might have explored her stomach area at one time. In bed I gazed at the ceiling, as if seeing it truly for the first time. Boy, that had been some trump card. A week later Uncle Buford threw Pancho out of his house.

No one ever found out the exact reason why he was banished. There were rumors of Pancho forging Uncle Buford's signature to checks, of lying to him when caught red-handed, and of cursing his uncle in front of grownups. But these didn't seem like strong enough reasons. It was actually hard to imagine any reason strong enough for good old Uncle Buford to toss Pancho out, a nephew who had grown up in his house. It must have been a lulu, one of those rare affronts—different for all people—that one cannot allow, be it from a relative, boss, anybody. It was so bad that it could not be articulated.

Pancho could not move in with me, where doors were barricaded at night and the womenfolk could sniff out liquor on someone's breath through a ton of Sen-Sen. He moved in bag and baggage with the Sheik, playing his hole card. Before, it had always been a refuge where he could stay a night or two during the week, flying to Uncle Buford's when he got on the Sheik's nerves but always being able to count on it. Now there was no place to fly to—except the streets. He had to make a go of it. And for the first few days Pancho was the model of the considerate boarder. He washed his hands before meals, let the Sheik tell his car-pool jokes without interruption, and performed all household chores without bragging. Evelyn said she thought Pancho's break with Uncle Buford might sober him up for life. But then he began to slip, in little, hardly noticeable ways at first. At the dinner table one night—I was there dodging the boardinghouse fare—Pancho suddenly snickered, looking at the Sheik, and said, "A family man."

"How's that?" The Sheik was taking a third helping of mashed potatoes, glancing around for something else.

"Aw, nothing."

"I thought it was nothing. Nothing is what always comes out of your mouth. Hey, Evelyn, is all the roast beef gone? Now somebody's eating like a hog around here."

Pancho snickered.

"Here you go, son," Momma Wilson said. "You take what's on my plate. I'm not that hungry, and I know you're working hard these days. Lord, a boy's got to keep his strength up."

"Thanks, Momma Wilson," he said, beaming.

Once Pancho had been staring at the Sheik sitting in the deep easy chair, nothing else, just looking at him with an amused glint in his dark eyes, stroking his chin, lips pursed. "O.K., Pancho," the Sheik said, throwing the sports section aside, "get that smirk off your face. Quit looking at me that way!"

Pancho lasted at the Sheik's house for nearly a month, up until Evelyn's pregnancy was near its end. I dropped by the house a short time after the explosion, unawares, carrying a cold six-pack and looking for a few laughs. The Sheik caught me on the front porch, shaking me by the shoulders as he hadn't done since moving into respectability and marriage. "Guess what I caught *him* doing? Just guess, guess!"

"What?"

"Fucking Momma Wilson!"

Seven

Pancho slept in cars for a time after that, sweet-talking Jujube at high school into letting him shower and shave in the gym's locker room. And under the most difficult circumstances he was still able to pull off a caper or two and show defiance. At a banquet in the Andrew Jackson honoring athletes who had set records in town Pancho managed to finger, under cover of the white tablecloth, the blonde, sexy wife of a prominent dentist. He just got his hand under there, like that, and began fingering away. Through the benediction, a speech by the mayor, and an inspirational message from a former star athlete sentenced to life in a wheel chair. He only let go long enough to receive a bronze plaque himself, honoring the fantastic number of touchdown passes he had once caught. Then back to the fingerwork, while the woman smiled idiotically at the ceiling.

And then the story went around that Pancho was slipping in the second-floor bedroom of another married woman right after her husband left for work at a shoe store. He would wedge a ladder under the window, run up and do his business, and then scurry down. The wife had been in our high school class, I remembered, a dimpled girl who liked red Jell-O with whipped cream during cafeteria lunch. Her husband—a quiet, plodding sort who'd been a plunging fullback on the high school squad—supposedly caught Pancho coming down the rungs once. He tore up the ladder with an ax and shamefully moved, with his wife in tow, to Detroit to work in an automobile plant.

Profligacy turned out to be another field Pancho had moved into, and he gave himself totally to it. From then on anyone in town who went off the deep end would have to be compared with Pancho. He was the champ. Rubber checks turned up all over under his hand, IOU's written in blood went unpaid, and the sheriff apprehended him once—revolver drawn—fornicating with a Roxy waitress in somebody else's car. Finally, though, the avenues closed for him in town and there was no place left to hide or cause a scene. He called me from a filling station on the highway that led out of town and asked if he could borrow five dollars. "Boney, I need it. I really do. Help me out."

"I'll see what I can do." I had saved some money on what my mother had given me to buy new shoes. With great presence of mind, I secured a few dollars in a hidden compartment of my wallet and left with only a five out on display.

On the oil-splattered pavement before the filling station pumps he stood with an odd grin in a torn T-shirt and old khaki pants. It was the same garb he liked to wear when driving past Meredith's house late at night in Uncle Buford's V-8. "You got it?" he said, right away.

"Here," opening my wallet.

"Thanks," he said, pocketing it, his grin turning to the smirk the Sheik hated so much. "What took you so long?"

"Hunh?" I wanted to hit him. Goddamn, he could be irritating. I'd walked three miles.

"Listen, Boney," he said, noticing my expression, "when you go to Europe, you'll take me with you, won't you? You promised, remember?"

I laughed uncomfortably, and then we both looked at each other, shrugging and throwing our hands out to the side, nothing left to say or do. His teeth had gone bad now, I saw, and his face had that gauntness you find on Tennessee hill people who have grown old before their time. You see it in Walker Evans' photographs. I left him on the highway that led to all those small towns in Kentucky and West Virginia where no one would know you and where a dishwasher's job was always open.

The Sheik went through three changes of mood as soon as Pancho had left town. "Good riddance," he said, at first. He told of how he had punched Pancho out the front door, had held him over the porch rail, choking him, and then had kicked him away. He liked to dwell on what might have happened, too. "I could have *killed* him. When I had my hands around his throat I came within a hair of it. That vein was popping out—and he was babbling out some sort of shit. I should have squeezed the goddamn life out of the son of a bitch . . ."

But as soon as it became clear Pancho wasn't coming

215

back to town for awhile—or couldn't—the Sheik's mood changed. "If he'd *only* pulled that stunt someplace else, then it wouldn't have been so bad at all. Why, who cares what goes on just as long as you don't know nothing about it? He was crazy for letting me catch him. He should have been more careful."

And after Evelyn had the baby, he moved into his final thoughts on Pancho. "Now why doesn't that crazy bastard come back to town? He thinks I'm mad at him, Boney. Why, hell, everybody has disagreements, but you don't run off and sulk forever over it. He can come back to stay here anytime. Only I don't want him fucking Momma Wilson—at least in public. He'll come back, don't you think so, Boney?"

The Sheik related dreams in which Pancho showed up, and all of us went down to the Buffalo just like in the old days. The dreams were so realistic, according to the Sheik, that he awoke certain Pancho was on the way. Once or twice Pancho did call the Sheik on the phone in the middle of the night. "Boney, guess what? The phone rings last night and this spooky voice comes on. I can tell somebody's got a handkerchief over the mouthpiece." He laughed, shaking his head. "This voice says, deep down, 'Sheik, I'm coming to get you. I'm going to cut your nuts off.' Hell, that's Pancho. I say, 'You crazy bastard, I could recognize that voice anyplace. Cut this foolishness out. Come on back to town. I'm not mad at you anymore. Come on back!' Then the line goes dead. But he's out there some place. He's coming back!"

The phone was not the only thing to awake the Sheik now in the middle of the night. The Baby screamed and screamed. Night and day. There I'd be, sitting in the living room, drawing on a can of beer, wanting to get into a poolroom yarn, when a shriek would pierce the air. Could that baby yell. And then, before you had half prepared yourself, it might be tossed into your arms like a football. What then? Its face would be a mass of wrinkles, turning the angry red of a boiled lobster. I rocked it as I'd seen others do, afraid it was going to pee, and then sailed it to the Sheik. He didn't mind holding it and bouncing it up and down, didn't object to stuffing a bottle in its mouth while he himself swigged a brew—what finally broke him, in the end, was changing its pants. "Ghazi," Evelyn would say, "you change the diapers this time. I've done it the last four times."

"I can't!"

"You've got to, simply got to. There are going to be times when I'm not here and you must." She was continually instructing him in the absolutely necessary duties of marriage; the frivolities she intelligently left alone, like flowers, and anniversaries remembered. *"You must!"*

The Sheik did not go around the bend in the way I would have imagined. He stopped eating, saying there was a pain in his side that ballooned every time he swallowed a bite. He was positive it was cancer. The doctor he went to diagnosed the ailment, though, as something to do with his back. From there he went to a chiropractor, who, after a few visits, managed to put a permanent crick in the Sheik's neck. He then had to wear a neck brace, his head lifted stiffly, his eyes rolling wildly from side to side. He drove in the car pool with the harness on his neck, and it was on when he added the long numbers at work. His clothes began to hang on him.

And he was angelically quiet those times I visited him, letting me tell my stories, never upset about anything. It happened one Saturday afternoon, a time in the past when we would be playing football or running racks at the Buffalo. The Baby screamed as it had from the start, but this time the Sheik stood, ripped off his neck brace, and fled. *"I can't take baby shit no more!"*

He ran to the only doctor he hadn't been to before in his

lifelong quest for proof of cancer—a Filipino who was new to town. The Sheik had burst past a startled receptionist and into his inner sanctum, walking in on the man giving a prostate massage to the president of the First National Bank. Everyone began wailing, the story went, the Filipino in a tongue no one could understand. The Sheik was crying by now, and the bank president said, "Whatever it is, son, go to your preacher. Go to a minister of the Lord."

"Oh, yes, sir, yes, sir. Why hadn't I thought of that before? Thank you, thank you."

He rushed into the study, he told me later, of the Methodist minister. Since Evelyn was of that faith, he thought he was required to go there. The minister was a tall, imposing man with the deep, melodic voice of an actor; he'd delivered many prayers before football games. He was writing something— possibly the sermon for the next day—when the Sheik came in crying and mumbling. He stood calmly, as if this was an everyday occurence, people appearing all the time with this kind of dilemma. He walked over and put his hand authoritatively on the Sheik's shoulder, eyes sad and understanding.

"Help me," the Sheik said. "Just tell me what to do. I can't take baby doo-doo anymore."

"Let us pray," the minister said, dropping to his knees.

The Sheik hit him, and backed away to the door. "Suck ass," he screamed, and ran. He ran to the highway and kept running until his breath gave out. Then he walked back home because he knew of no place else that would take him. Everyone in town then considered him insane—and made the necessary allowances. Humor him, don't make him angry. Cross the street when you see him coming. No one was put away in our town unless he actually killed somebody, and sometimes not even then. The Sheik worked his job the best he could,

218

hanging on by his fingernails—and sired five more children. Each time was easier, he said. But not much.

I sympathized with him during his breakdown in a special way because I now had a new confinement of my own. Someone had miraculously hired me for a job. I sat behind a desk near the plate glass of an office downtown, the first line of defense against people lumbering in from the street, acting as a sort of Good Humor Man. After the initial bold stroke of hiring me, my boss, who was a good fellow not much older than I, had trouble focusing his eyes on me and specifying what I should do. He liked to stand in the middle of the office, jiggling the change in his pants and getting in a little pocket pool, too, I suspected, his head turning nervously for a glance or two at the willowy, married brunette of a secretary. Her husband was a tough-looking dude who drove a truck and picked her up after work. He looked as if he could break you in two. So hands off, except in fancy.

My first chore of the day was to give my boss a weather forecast. "Looks like rain this afternoon," I would say.

"Uh, well," a masterful pocket-pool shot, the secretary having crossed her silken legs, "yes and no. Rain would be good for the farmers around . . ."

He never finished sentences, and relished long sessions in his private office alone with the door closed. I read the wall clock, read the paper (three of them, cover to cover), sharpened tens of thousands of pencils, cherished and hoarded and extended to its utmost limits the most mundane and routine of reports and puerile charts. I savored the coffee break as if it were pheasant under glass. First came a glance or two at the magazines in the coffee shop, then squirming up on a stool, the banter with the sawed-off waitress, and finally slurping the bitter coffee that turned gray with a squirt of condensed milk —no need blessedly to look busy now. The community john was another refuge, and—trying not to seem too peculiar or kidney damaged—I shuffled there when no one was looking. Locked in a stall, my head in my hands, I would feel tears running down my cheeks. The sheer boredom and uselessness and endlessness of office work. I moaned—and if anyone caught me, a foot suddenly appearing, I pretended the throes of a bowel movement. "Oh, God, oh, God, help me. . . ."

The World Series on the air helped; also, a murder/rape to follow in the papers. And after the most valiant effort, of pleading with the wall clock, sweating its every inch forward, interspersed with imagery of the willowy secretary suddenly raising her skirt and straddling my shoulders, five o'clock would strike. It was then as if a coin had been dropped in a Wurlitzer and "Colonel Bogey's March" had come on. Out the door I would sail, a spring in my step, head high with great purposefulness. Escape. And a car salesman along Market Street caught that look of the gainfully employed on my face one day, and sold me a new sedan. It didn't matter that I had nothing to put down. The First National was overjoyed to make a loan. I had a job.

Now I gathered up the clan after work for the spin to the boardinghouse meal, the shame of Yellow Cab transport in abeyance. Sometimes in my quitting-time euphoria I would barrel off with someone half-in, half-out of the car, usually my father who would be screaming. Or I'd overlook someone—my aunt, say—and have to backtrack from the boardinghouse for her. And all along the way my mother would be pointing out sights: "Oh, isn't that a lovely house, look at those charming flowers . . ."

On weekends I washed and simonized the car, even painting the tires with a shiny black substance that Montgomery-Ward sold. It made no difference that the car had no real place to go, it was truly mine (forget the bank) after all those years of fantasy. At night I would steal to the side window for just another peek, marveling at its wax glistening in the moonlight, its chrome like diamonds. Mine, mine. And then back to lounge in the living room where we looked at one another in exhaustion. Escape? I had obligations, staggering bank payments to make each month.

In other words, I had joined the American work force.

But that highway did lead out of town. People had broken free of tighter chains; they had escaped from Devil's Island, hadn't they? And somewhere in life there must be more excitement waiting than a coffee break and a pocket-pool shot at an off-limits secretary—else how could a Mozart symphony have been written or a Thackeray novel?

And on a double date I met the strangest girl, someone who gave me a hint of what lay elsewhere. (Now with a car the field had been reversed so that I was the one to give other people lifts; she was the other guy's date.) And what surprises! She was so pretty with a mass of dark hair, blue-green eyes, and a soft girlish voice. In wonder then I watched her pick up a cue stick in the roadhouse we went to and try out some shots on an old back room table. She sat on the table once, her fine muscled legs sticking out (I noted), and made a perfect straight-in from behind her back. A pretty girl, like that, with such a soft trill to her voice. And the wonders didn't end there. Suddenly she just broke into a Charlie Chaplin imitation—for no reason, just did it, twirling the cue stick around as if it were a bamboo cane. And then, at the booth, she picked up a cigar and began smoking it. "Ummm, mild," she said, flipping it up and down between her teeth and moving her eyebrows like Groucho Marx.

And she said *fuck,* a nice girl, actually did without the Reverend Dr. Lovelace rushing in with a whistle and the sheriff with a shotgun. My head was spinning. Back in the car she took the pint that was offered her and drank it straight, shaking her head to get it down. What a marvelous girl had just been waiting here in town, waiting for me as my shiny sedan had been in the car lot. For weeks after that night I tried getting a date with her. Finally she gave in, and I raced over. We saw a movie, had a bar-be-cue, did everything you're supposed to do on a date—and at the end, parked in front of her house, I grabbed her breast. She slapped me. "No man does that to me!" but added, in a stagey Scarlett O'Hara voice, "Suh."

Her name was Juanita. I fell in love with her, and she gave me my manhood and enough courage to leave. To go so far that I left her. Or her me. Something. But wouldn't there always be plenty of Juanitas around now that I had become a man?

Yes, there are bigger ball games out there. From the sidelines at Shea I have watched Joe Namath throw a forty-yard touchdown pass to Maynard with three-hundred-pound Ernie Ladd coming down on his head. And girls? Let me tell you. Just a stroll to the corner kiosk and a new one pops up. They wear bikini underpants these days, striped like candy, which they like to wash at your place and hang up to dry overnight. They don't wear brassieres, don't need to because their breasts are so firm or (poignantly) so small. They are actresses, models, dancers, and painters—sometimes the whole works rolled into one, a delight often from the Bronx, who also admits shyly that she's a poet. They are forever in transit—off to

California, to hitchhike through the Near East, to live in a commune in New Mexico. While her place is still warm in bed, she might be five hundred miles out over the Atlantic. Flaming post cards from verdant spots take up half the mailbox. Sometimes I wonder—why so many? To prove I'm not queer?

Well, it must be the most enjoyable way on earth to prove it, far preferable to joining the marines. But there come the bad moments inevitably, the real shockers. The one who looked so fetching at the party—a bridge of freckles over her nose, a Huck Finn cap, a dimpled smile. In your apartment you turn your back and she's shooting dope in her little toe or jumping out the window. And then there are those who stick around a little longer than usual, perhaps even to feed you soup when you have the flu. Then in bed, in the dead of night, she finds it's time to confide. She tells you she has fucked her dad, mom, sis, four brothers, and even let the collie get in his licks. But we can't, of course. The trauma from the recent abortion, you know. I stare bug-eyed at the ceiling for the rest of the night. Did I rush to leave—for *this?* What happened to the Mozart symphonies?

I then go back occasionally to try to see actually why I did leave so long ago. The Sheik catches me every time, maniacally interested in what I can tell him about Joe Namath. Joe is his hero, a dark-skinned lad who'd played at the University of Alabama, suffering in the Sheik's mind because his father was from the old country, was from peasant stock, but who had claimed victory in the end. Shown them all. In the Super Bowl.

"Boney," he says, "now don't tell me any lies. I want to know the truth. Is Joe getting all that pussy they say he is?" I open my mouth, but before a word comes out, he grabs my

223

shoulders the way he used to on the vacant lot and shakes me. "Why, you know goddamn well he is!"

Pancho never came back. Meredith Lancaster married a man from out of town, someone I've been told who beats her. Her son is a star football player.